ON A BENDER

ON A BENDER

Eduardo Blanco Amor

Translated by Craig Patterson

Planet

Published
in Wales in 2012
by Planet

PO Box 44
Aberystwyth
Ceredigion SY23 3ZZ
Cymru/Wales

Cover, typesetting
and design: Dafydd Prys

Printed by Gwasg Gomer
Llandysul, Ceredigion

The publisher acknowledges the financial
support of the Welsh Books Council

ISBN: 978-0-9540881-9-4

Translator's acknowledgements

The translation into English of Eduardo Blanco Amor's novel, *A Esmorga*, would not have been possible without the assistance, support and criticism of a number of people. I would like to thank the following friends, colleagues and institutions for their help with bringing the project to fruition:

Luis González Tosar, who on behalf of the PEN Club of Galicia and the Deputación de Ourense first offered me the honour of translating this idiosyncratic work of Galician fiction. Victor Freixanes, Montse Sousa and Xosé Soutullo at Galaxia, and Helle Michelsen, Jasmine Donahaye and Dafydd Prys at Planet, for all their support. David MacKenzie and X.L. Regueira for ongoing support and advice on a number of translation challenges. Xosé Manuel Dasilva for his assistance with Blanco Amor's vocabulary, and his recovery of segments of the novel removed by Franco's censors, which enables this edition to be the first translation into any language of the fully-restored text. Sarah Aldred, Philip R. Davies and Eva Moreda for kindly reading the draft text and offering me invaluable feedback. Xesús Fraga, Ana Couceiro, Dani and Leda, for putting a roof over my head, a computer in front of me, superb food inside me, and for making me feel as always like one of the family in Betanzos during that eventful summer of 2009 when most of the important groundwork for the translation was completed. A note of special thanks must go to Xesús Fraga for providing constant support, feedback, criticism and suggestions during the entirety of the project (and indeed for passing it on to me). Finally, my deepest gratitude must be expressed to Xabier Cid, whose local knowledge of Auria and infinite patience with regard to my enquiries enabled the translation to be completed in the first place, and with such fidelity.

Introduction

Eduardo Blanco Amor was born in Ourense, Galicia, in 1897. He was the youngest, sickly son of a family of modest means that was abandoned by the father three years later. Without a formal education and largely self-taught, Blanco Amor was heavily involved in the cultural and intellectual life of his hometown by his late teens, and at this time witnessed the emergence of the Galician cultural nationalist movement.

For several centuries, Galician-language culture had largely lain dormant in the stagnation that followed internal colonisation. Unlike the case of Catalonia, Galician was not the language of commerce or social prestige, but had survived the centuries following the subjugation of Galicia by Castile and the Catholic monarchs in the late medieval period by being spoken by the peasantry, farmers and fishermen. It received a timely stimulus with the advent of Romanticism, which filtered into the northwest of the Iberian Peninsula most notably through the poetry of Rosalía de Castro in the 1860s. The late nineteenth century saw several literary and cultural figures reassert a distinctive Galician identity through poetry and historiography, a movement known as the *Rexurdimento* (rebirth). It was this legacy that was inherited by the generation of writers, scholars and politicians based in Ourense during the first decades of the twentieth century. Known as the *Xeración Nós* (Generation Us), they were Blanco Amor's intellectual and ideological mentors. During the 1920s and '30s, they consolidated Galician literature's revival after several centuries of marginalisation and repression, in spite of the restrictions placed on cultural expression by the Primo de Rivera dictatorship (1923-1930), and the political instability of the Spanish Second Republic that followed.

They continued Galicia's poetic tradition, developed journalism, produced theatre and pioneered the essay in the native language. Crucially they brought the Galician-language novel to new heights of aesthetic maturity.

Galicia remains one of the poorer corners of the Spanish state, cut off from development and opportunity by land, resources, and political influence, but in contact with the wider world via the Atlantic. Like many other western peripheries, Galicia experienced widespread emigration in the nineteenth and twentieth centuries, mostly to Latin America, especially to Argentina and, to a lesser extent, Cuba, Uruguay and Brazil. Blanco Amor took the most common route of Galician emigration when he travelled to Buenos Aires in 1919. He founded Galician cultural magazines among the emigrant community in the Argentinian capital, published his first novel in 1927, and his first poetry collection in 1928. In that year, he made the return crossing to Galicia as a foreign correspondent for the Argentinian press, and resumed direct contact with the burgeoning Galician cultural and literary scene. He met Castelao, the leader of Galician nationalism, and submitted contributions to Galician literary publications. He returned once more to Spain 1933, when he met Federico García Lorca in Madrid, developing a friendship that would prove crucial for the propagation of Galician culture. Lorca, whose plays and poetry project a southern Spanish identity and affirm Andalusian identity against the dominant metropolitan tradition, was fascinated by Galician culture. Lorca's *Seis poemas galegos* (1935) – six poems written in Galician by Spain's most prominent artist at the time – owes much to the influence of Blanco Amor who was also instrumental in getting the collection published. It was the only occasion that Lorca wrote in a language other than Castilian.

Blanco Amor and Lorca were also both homosexual writers from opposite ends of the Iberian Peninsula who experienced understandable frustrations within an essentially Catholic and conservative culture. Lorca was one of the first high-profile victims of the violence that erupted with the Spanish Civil War in 1936. From Argentina, Blanco Amor defended the legitimacy of the Second Republic against the right-wing military uprising led by the Galician, General Franco. However, there was little more he could do, apart from aiding Galician exiles (such as Castelao) fleeing from political persecution and in many cases certain death in Spain, while contributing to the survival of Galician culture from afar. Blanco Amor's decision to write in Castilian for the next twenty years was by no means an isolated phenomenon on either side of the Atlantic; even though in Galicia itself, the much weakened Galician cultural and political movement survived in a limited way when it was not entirely suppressed by a regime that had murdered many of its leading figures. Blanco Amor returned to Galician as a language of literary composition in the late 1950s, ending the decade with the novel that is most closely associated with him and which has become a classic of Galician literature, A Esmorga (On a Bender). He continued to work in education, theatre, journalism and literature among the Galician emigrant community in Buenos Aires, before returning definitively to Spain in 1965. The last fourteen years of his life were the most productive in his career, coinciding with the somewhat relaxed censorship during the final decade of the Franco regime. He died in Vigo in 1979, and is buried in Ourense.

Many of his works are set in the fictional city of Auria, a literary representation of his native Ourense, but none has quite captured the Galician imagination as much as A Esmorga: Galicians consistently name it in surveys as the best Galician novel ever written. The term 'esmorga' in Galician refers to a prolonged bout of drinking and general shenanigans, and the novel centres on one such extended binge among three friends which culminates in tragedy. Its main characters are all marginalised in one way or another, and its impact and resonance lie in its stark and unflinching portrayal of violence, sexuality, illness (both physical and mental), and extremes of human behaviour. It is also a landmark in Galician culture because it contains the first overtly homosexual character(s) in Galician literature. Some critics have suggested Camus' *L'Étranger* (1942) and *La Chute* (1956) as possible influences on a narrative consisting of monologues in the voice of a stranger, though *La Chute* was in fact published a year after *A Esmorga* was written, as Blanco Amor himself pointed out. A more likely influence can be found closer to home in the novels of Camilo José Cela, the Galician-born writer and Nobel Prize winner who wrote in Castilian and was part of the *tremendismo* (coarse realism) movement in Spanish literature in the 1940s and '50s which sought to shake up post-Civil War fiction and shock its audience into a change of social outlook. In his first novel, *La familia de Pascual Duarte* (1942), the eponymous narrator-protagonist recounts in rural dialect his criminal life before execution. There are clear parallels here with Cibrán's declaration before the judge, which is the central narrative strand in *On a Bender*, delivered in the colloquial dialect of Ourense: an earthy and coarse Galician which heightens the work's intensity and authenticity. *A Esmorga* renewed Galician prose during a crucial period of cultural and linguistic resistance. The novel it is set near the end of the nineteenth century, but its confessional style, together with its theme of the nature of truth and the ways in which truth can be manipulated before an authority whose repression is all the more sinister because of its muted, ambiguous nature, left contemporary readers in no doubt of its implicit criticism of the Franco regime.

Blanco Amor wrote *A Esmorga* in five months. It was his first attempt at a novel in Galician, a genre that was still not that common in the mid 1950s. The manuscript was taken to Galicia from Argentina by Isaac Díaz Pardo on behalf of Blanco Amor at the end of 1955, and handed to the Galician-language publisher, Galaxia, which then began the process of submitting it to the Francoist censor. The first attempt at publication in Galicia in 1956 was rejected on the grounds of its obscene language rather than for political reasons. After some further difficulties, Blanco Amor followed a course familiar to many writers who could not get their work past the censors, and sought publication in Latin America. *A Esmorga* appeared in Buenos Aires on 3 April, 1959. The novel was submitted to the censor on two further occasions in 1969 in a new attempt to get it published in Galicia. Although the literary quality of the work was recognised on this occasion, it was nonetheless cut in five places in order to suppress criticism of authority, including the reference at the end to the possible causes of the protagonist's death. It was finally published in Galician in December 1970. In 2010, Galaxia published a restored version which retained the five fragments suppressed by the censor over forty years earlier. *On a Bender* is the first translation of *A Esmorga* into English and the first translation of the newly-restored version in any language.

Craig Patterson

DOCUMENTATION

When I was still a young boy, the episode continued to be discussed by the good people of Auria – the city where I was born and where those things had happened. It would be recounted in many different ways, all of which coincided in the ending, which was always the same.

Later, when I was older and discovered the habit of writing, I spoke to those people who had been around at that time, asking questions here and there. I poked into papers and read the old local journals that I found heaped up in messy piles and lightly nibbled by mice in the attic of the Gentlemen's Club. This was the centre of gatherings for the powers that be and the Maragato merchants from the north León region. As they were all fervent card players, they had no passion for local chronicles that could be turned into history or literature, and for the same reason were devoid of all inclination to compile archives that went beyond their accounts and proceedings.

An uncle of mine, who had been a 'minister' at the magistrate's court (in his day they would call the bailiffs by that unfortunate name), never wanted to talk to me about the episode, at least not in an impromptu manner, even though he was without doubt the person who was best acquainted with it among those who were still alive. But when I was a boy he would not say a thing, and later I began to see that he had been entirely right about that. Only when he saw that I was a sensitive, mature lad who was acquainted with some great books (in spite of my parents being minded to direct me towards the Honoured Guild of Cabinet Makers), and dallying with the posh students, did he begin to tell me little by little (like someone paying out a sum of money) what he had seen and heard of this story about the three famous revellers, which was a tragic tale at heart, even though it would sometimes be told in a light-hearted way in the bars.

At that time my uncle was already an old man and his memory was failing him, and although he had once been a renowned raconteur, much in demand and listened to in get-togethers and inns, old age made him stutter. The jugs of wine that I had to get him to boost his spirits and pep him up were endless, as well as the odd drop of sweet brandy on cold evenings. On many an afternoon I had to take him out to enjoy the sun along the A Granxa road, whose bars, redolent with fine country plonk, soothed the melancholy of the pensioners. I made all these sacrifices because I was trying to make events come alive in a way that the court papers, with their soporific prose and familiar distortions, did not succeed in doing, or which the now traditional yarns told around town succeeded in doing only too well.

I also had to avail myself of Silverscissors, who was a tailor and son of another tailor who had been a fellow stitcher of Menaplenty, who the reader will meet in due course and forever be angry with, or at least I assume so, although I suppose that our tastes may differ here. Apparently in his old age the father of this other tailor did nothing but talk about the matter. He would recount the events in twenty or thirty different ways, depending on how the mood took him as the story developed, but always with great personal and lively enthusiasm, as if instead of being a contemporary, a mere contemporary like so many others who half a century ago now (for in my town people live with unending persistence) had taken part in the events, he had been one of the leading protagonists. Because of all of this, I took such second-hand accounts (although second-stitch accounts would be a better way of putting it) to be far too suspect, far too imaginative and detailed, as is often the case with the accounts of tailors who agonise over the decorative meticulousness and the sedentary preciosity that befits their profession.

So, picking up things here and there and giving some of my own thought to it, and with only glimpses of the characters to go on, I now begin to write this account: almost forty years after gathering such scarce documentation, and ninety after the events themselves. That is why it will be all too easy to detect some blemishes where the objective truth is concerned, as is always the case with the realist formulas to which this manuscript consciously adheres, its author acknowledging in advance the usual outrage and vilification that may follow from such a declaration.

CHAPTER ONE

'...'

'No, Sir, it didn't happen like it says on that bit of paper that they've read out, 'cause paper only tells what they've got written down on it, though I didn't understand very much of that anyway. The gentleman here read it in such a hurry, and besides that we're not used to hearing Castilian being read out loud 'cause we don't speak it here, and whenever someone who isn't a gentleman begins to speak it, we tell him that he's speaking Castrapo, that he's mixing Galician and Castilian... But at the end of the day that's not what really happened, even though the Civil Guard, old Esquilacha or the Pope himself may say so, begging your pardon. Not the start of things, nor what came afterwards, nor the end. Nobody knows anything 'cause nobody saw anything, and if they did see it they didn't notice, 'cause seeing is one thing and noticing another.'

'...'

'As I said, and they didn't write this down, I was going to work. I was going to work, and I swear to God that I had never left my house, or Raxada's house, which for the record is the same thing, so set on going to work. On Saturday, Raxada had gone to meet me at the worksite and we made up for her sake 'cause I love her a lot, but even more so for the little one who's now almost four, and 'cause he's so bright, he's starting to understand things about life... I slept with her on Saturday and Sunday too, and didn't half need to, 'cause there's no shortage of women out there, but women like her, well at least as far as I'm concerned... With one thing and another, she rabbited on so much that... As it was so cold and with us sleeping huddled up together, I had no choice but to listen to her, and apart from that she was right... And she rabbited on so much that she made me weep like no woman ever did, except for my mother, 'cause though mothers can make us men weep, it's no reason for a man to feel ashamed. And she ended up being right in what she said, just as she was often right in what she did with bits of her body, 'cause I can't keep away from her for very long, no matter what Skinny does, and she knows a thing or two... Apart from all that, Raxada has a certain way with words, 'cause she drops them gently into your ear and it's almost as if they were just her breathing at times... And she told me about herself and the kid and things about this bastard world, begging your pardon...

'Well now, after the things that tend to happen when a man and a woman sleep together happened, and if you're young and things happen once and then a second time, and then again and again, 'cause we'd been without nooky for a month, well you gradually forget little by little what to do with yourself when you're flat out like that in a woman's arms. When it's with the others, I clear off quickly 'cause I even reckon they seem to start to stink and smell quite rough, if you'll excuse me. But with Raxada, you stay in the warmth of her bed and slowly turn into a little kid, snuggled up against that wide and lovely bosom of hers, as if she were your mother, even though she's younger than...

'But apart from all that, she was more than right. It wasn't the kid's fault for being born or that his mother was a whore and his father a drunkard... A drunkard but not a layabout, if we're being honest about things... There was the poor blighter hunched up at the foot of the bed, in a bundle of rags and old blankets. Whenever I lit the candle to go and do my business, he would open his eyes, which are surly and blue just like his granny's, and give me a smile. He would go to sleep and wake up every so often, nibbling on the fritters that I'd brought him. And once I even had to get up to scare away a mouse for him that was getting stuck into them, and I gave him a slug of that wine with rosemary and sugar that we had warming on the fire place. One of those times the innocent little bugger asked me:

'"Why do you hit Mummy?"

'"I don't hit her. Why do you say that?"

'"'Cause she moans. I heard her moaning quietly."

'Youngsters spot everything, damn it… And I told him:

'"Now now, go to sleep, go on to sleep…"

'I asked him if he was cold, and do you know what he told me?

'"When you're here I'm not cold, even if I'm not sleeping in the bed…" 'Cause my boy is a bright one, you know, and sometimes he says things that send shivers up your spine, so much that I wish he wouldn't speak like grown-ups do. Subela has often told me that that's his mother's trying to soften me up, but that isn't true, 'cause they say that when I was a kid I'd say that kind of thing too. 'Cause my boy, little Lisardo…'

'…'

'Yes, Sir, yes, I'm getting to the point. I'm doing nothing else, even though it doesn't seem like that. In men's lives, even men like me, not everything is done on the hoof, 'cause things need to have their beginning, and often what you see comes out of what you didn't see, and you have to keep saying everything, even though at the start it doesn't seem to be relevant… And getting to the point, the point is that Mr Pepito, the doctor, had told me that Raxada's ailment, though it's not easy to spot first thing, is one of those that can cripple you if it's not looked after, and I had to help her out so that things didn't get worse… Help her and my son, otherwise they were going to take him to the Sisters' Orphanage, where they all come out with rickets in no time at all. And no matter how damaged you might be in the deepest depths of your soul, you don't have a child just for them to toss him onto a pile of horse shit, begging your pardon, or for them to suck the joy out of him by keeping them just as they do in the shadows of the children's home, gulping down hot water with stale, second-hand bread and whispering Hail Marys all the while like they were passing judgment. Poor little sod!'

'…'

'Yes, Sir, yes, I'll carry on now. Give me a few seconds to get it together, 'cause with that matter of… my voice gets all hoarse… and… Right then, as I've been saying, I wasn't out on the piss, as it wasn't the time to be out on the piss unless you've already been on it all night long. I was heading off to my job at the works along the new road. I'd already been there for five months or so since the summer, ever since the works had come up from Alongos. I've already said this, everybody knows it and I shouldn't have to repeat it. I get a good day's pay, about one and a half pesetas from one day to another, turning boulders into gravel from dawn to dusk. There are worse jobs and I can't complain… The shack where Raxada has lived since she left Monfortina's place because of the little one was left to her by her parents with a bit of land around it, which she sold when she went on the game. It's past Mariñamansa, so I had to leave when it was still dark in order to be in Ervedelo at seven in the morning, which is along where they are bringing the highway, as you Sir have pointed out, and I work there beside the bridge that they are putting up as quick as can be so that the MP can get through, who they say is coming next month for the elections… Poor old Raxada had made me some garlic soup, which I could still feel warming my cockles when I left, begging your pardon, and I felt the morning chill that ran through my whole body, as if the soup was the only warm thing that I had inside, God help me. It'd been freezing over all night, and the mud was hard on the cart tracks, and the highway seemed like stone, and you could even slip on the pools left by the rain just as if they were made of thick glass, and even the grass by the ditch shone with the frost as if it were lit from below ground, 'cause you could still hardly see a thing.

'I was walking with my feet all stricken with chilblains that ran through all the joints of my feet, begging your pardon, and they bloody hurt when I knocked with my clogs against the bumps in the road, so I had to go along the grass, which though not soft, was softer than the rock-hard frozen mud. As well as my feet bothering me, Raxada had gone over the top with the pepper in the soup and had made it all hot, so my stomach was going from being hot to burning me up... And what with all that and so much graft the night before, I was going to work in a very bad mood, and I was itching to find a bar open where I could have a few little glasses of white, 'cause I might be whatever they say I am, but I'm not like others who have half a dozen shots of firewater for breakfast, you know, country augardente.

'After walking for a bit, and as I was reaching the inn known as Cristalina's place, the weather eased up all of a sudden, with a mist as black as my sins which rose up from the south, but easier to tolerate than that razor-sharp cold that smacked me bang in the face when I was leaving my girl's house. High up in the sky, which was gently, almost lazily clearing up, some dark clouds were building, and you could see that a storm was brewing. I was beginning to see that it was going to mess up my day's work, but there was no decent excuse, not like on other occasions when I would latch onto anything in order not to go to the site. Now, even if I had to go crawling, I would keep to what I'd promised. I would ask the foreman to give me another job in the huts for the day, as the thing was to do your bit, and besides I still know something about blacksmithing, how to aim the borers'drills, pickaxes and the like.

'So I sank my hands into the pockets of my sheepskin jacket, clenching my teeth 'cause of the damned chilblains that would stick to my clogs and come unstuck again, and 'cause of my stomach that blazed away inside me like I had a heather stump burning away in it, I stomped along angrily. It was then, thinking about the "damned life of a working man" as Serantes says at those workers' gatherings that are now fashionable and are called "meetings", and he's quite right, even though he's no more than a chippy, that I happened to see in the distance, through the mist, the shapes of two men who looked like they were trying to blend in with the large elm trees that are down there beside the road. Only that didn't work, as one of them struck a match to light a cigarette, and smoke came off him and around his feet too, which made me realise that they were having a piss, begging your pardon, huddled up against the tree, and why with such caution I don't know as not a living soul could be seen, though perhaps they did that as it's a man's habit to do so even when nobody can see. So I stopped too to roll a cigarette and also to give them time to move on from there, as I don't like to go past people who don't show their faces like they should, nor to avoid them as if I were distrustful or afraid. So I started to walk slowly, flicking my lighter so they would notice me, though it was clear by now that they had seen or heard me hobbling along in my clogs, which are iron-shod, and even more when I started to walk along the middle of the road... And it was then that the men's two shapes emerged from the misty rain and came towards me, running and howling like two phantoms, with a blanket thrown over their heads and only their four feet to be seen. I figured straight away that it would be a prank by some acquaintances, but just to be on the safe side I grasped my knife in my hand and stood still. When they reached me they let the blanket slip as they broke into laughter, and it turned out to be Gobs and Menaplenty.'

'...'

'Yes, Sir, yes, the very same ones. Juan Fariña and Eladio Vilarchao, who are there on those papers in Castilian, are Gobs and Menaplenty by nickname, which is how we know everybody here and it doesn't offend anyone, as Juan and Eladio could be anybody, but Gobs and Menaplenty can only be who they are, in the same way that I am Cipriano Canedo and they call me Cibrán or Boar, or however Sir fancies, 'cause my father had a boar to sort out the sows, begging your pardon... Though they also call me Wormy and Rotten Top, 'cause when I was a lad I had ringworm, and it lasted till I was a young man, and I used to go about with my cap tightly on...'

'...'

'No, Sir, no. It was only for us to get to understand each other, as I'm starting to realise that you're not from round here...'

'...'

'No, Sir, no. It doesn't bother me, I'm just telling you so that you understand, as we had a foreman too who was from down Murcia way, and even when we spoke to him in his language he didn't understand us... Anyhow, getting back to the matter in hand, they were Juan Fariña, or Xanciño Gobs, or the Elephant, or the Big Man, and Eladio Vilarchao, or Menaplenty, or Daddy Big Stitch, or Seven Skirts, or the Fairy, or whatever Sir prefers, 'cause here we all have plenty to choose from... So they surrounded me, laughing and slapping me on the back, and Menaplenty pinching me in the privates just like he always bloody did, and wanting to put the blanket over me. I'd left them in Big Nose's pub two days ago, which was Saturday, at the start of one of those benders that had made them so famous among all the piss artists in Auria and roundabouts, and which they got into and didn't get out of until they collapsed somewhere, almost always in an alleyway or on a path on the edge of town where the locals or the police would grab them and throw them into the cells until their hangover had gone, or until their brothers went to ask after them, as both their brothers are working men with good heads on their shoulders, and they even felt ashamed for having such good-for-nothings in the family, though even the best families have their share of bad luck... And that's not to insult my friends or to stick anything on them that everybody doesn't already know, as they say.'

'...'

'Yes, Sir. Why would I deny it? I also got into those things on the odd occasion. But this time it wasn't like that. It wasn't, 'cause from the beginning of last week, God knows I had it in mind to make up with my... well, with Raxada, and give her my wages every Saturday so as not to fall into temptation. The truth is the truth. Perhaps I'm no better or worse than them, but in this case I had it in mind to act differently from then on, or to behave differently, which amounts to the same thing... So they grabbed me by the hands and spun me round with them, and made me laugh, and the three of us rolled about laughing, and above the laughter of the three of us could be heard the voice of Menaplenty, who sounds like a hen when he laughs, and that's why I don't like laughing with him when there are people around, 'cause it attracts attention. And a lot of the time, when we always used to hang around there, from one pub to another, I didn't laugh at all, just so that he wouldn't let out that woman's cackle that made everyone look at where it was coming from and take the piss out of us.

'It was easy to see that they were now, as they say, on the last legs of a good bender, but still quite drunk. Menaplenty put the blanket around his waist like a skirt, and started to dance, singing that Morrongo song, imitating some tart who had come to the Mendenúñez Café for the Corpus Christi fiestas. He danced around Gobs, pulling faces at him to look like a fusspot, and the other fella acted as if he were shooing someone away, like someone scaring off flies. Then he went towards Gobs and began pinching and tickling him, and the two laughed their heads off, and Menaplenty laughed through the top of his nose the way that a seamstress sniggers... Then they threw the blanket over themselves and began to natter on in Castrapo, imitating the way posh folk talk.

'"How are you, Sir?"

'"Very well thank you, although a tad pissed off with the temperature..." I don't know why, but when they said "temperature", they burst out laughing so much that it seemed as if they would choke.

'I hated all that (I'd told him so many times), and I began to walk off, on my way. But after taking a few steps, I heard Gobs let out a deafening cry, and I saw that the other fella had grabbed him by his privates, dying with laughter as he twisted them. But Gobs quickly recovered and bashed him in the middle of his chest with a wallop, which boomed just like a bomb going off and knocked Menaplenty flat out on the ground. You could see that at least Gobs wasn't that drunk, as drunkards' punches don't have that effect. When Menaplenty, without managing to get up, began to spit out those insults at him that he could choose so well to cause offence, the other fella jumped on top of him to lay in with kicks a second time.

He gave him a few until I got there and put myself between the two of them, and in my wanting to stop Gobs' onslaught, I almost got knocked down by him too, for I've never seen a bull like him, and besides, he's one of those who go mad when they start to lay into a man. So Menaplenty shut up and lay there, wailing in a childlike voice. It made me feel sorry for him and I didn't know what to do. Gobs was going from one side to another wobbling, his body all hunched up, swearing under his breath with his hands covering his genitals like anybody who was feeling great pain. I helped Aladio to get up and told them:

'"That's what happens when you can't hold your drink."

'"Pot kettle black," murmured Menaplenty, who would never shut up even if he were dying, and with that he put the blanket over his head and began to walk off.

'"Stop right there, you old shit…! As soon as I can get up I'm going to have your guts for garters, you bastard…!"

'"You'll get indigestion," cackled the other fella through that seamstress grin of his, and beginning to slope off in small steps that were all his short little legs could manage. Gobs suddenly stretched out, and in four strides had already knocked Menaplenty to the ground, and was on top of his back, hitting him savagely on his sides and with his teeth sunk into the nape of his neck, just like a rabid dog, save for his blessed soul. Menaplenty spun around, his lips chapped, without even the chance to complain… It took everything I had to separate them, and I still think that if I pulled it off, it was only 'cause at that moment a string of pack mules could be seen approaching, and we could hear the bells of the mules and the babble of the muleteers.

'Gobs got up on top of the other fella, wiping his mouth with his hand and spitting. The day was breaking very, very slowly, and was dirtied by the storm cloud. I felt ashamed that anybody might see them like that: one with his shirt all torn and his bloodied, and the other sprawled out face down on the floor, flat out like a dead man. But as far as they were concerned, they weren't to be taken too seriously. They were always knocking about like that, winding each other up, giving each other a hiding until one of them could stand it no longer, only for them to seek each other out again. It was never clear if they were fond of or hated each other, but they couldn't knock about without one another and I never saw them drunk on their own, as if to knock about together they had to drink. And when they weren't on a binge they didn't seem to even know one another, and hardly spoke to each other. Hello and goodbye, as if they were ashamed of each other. But as soon as they got together they did nothing but quarrel terribly. And the strangest thing is that if somebody mocked Menaplenty, then would go at them, and there were many scuffles that blew up because of Xanciño's habit of answering for that shameless hussy. Menaplenty, with his flabby, tubby look just like a pat of butter, couldn't take the weakest of punches, and made the most of this to cause that mayhem by taking the piss out of others, with that way of his of eyeballing people, his little grin and those words he'd dash out as if flicking paint on a wall, always looking for the spot where they'd cause most hurt: that's what he was made for. When they would say something to him as a joke about his trade as a tailor, "seven tailors don't make a man" or something like that, he would spit out such venom that you didn't know whether to put up with it or to belt him in the face a few times.

'So I got up again, grabbed the other fella by the sleeve and urged them to get into the ditch, which was quite deep at that point. I went back to the road just as the string of pack mules was passing by, and one of the horse dealers, who no doubt had glimpsed something of the scuffle , stopped me to ask for a light, keeping a wayward eye out for where the others had hidden.

'"Having fun, are we?" he said, grunting between drags.

'"It's nothing serious. Just Monday hangovers."

'"Just as well... But keep your eyes open. We came across a couple of Civil Guards having some shots of augardente in Seixalvo. Seems that they're all after someone who caused a right mess at an inn in town. They're coming here as relief guard. Anyway... cheers."

'"And to you."

'I kept quiet, letting the long line of mules go by, then whistled to the others, gesturing for them to come out, without moving from where I was, as the damned horse dealers kept looking back. As they weren't coming out of the hideout, I went over towards it, wondering if they were quietly finishing each other off, just as those drunkards who fight without saying a word do. There I found them – and I pray God I hadn't – just the opposite to what I was expecting. Xanciño was sat by the side of the ditch with the other fella, wailing, resting on his knees, wiping the wound on his neck with a cloth that he was dipping in a muddy pool. The wound wasn't deep, but caught the eye with its torn skin sunk into the holes made by the teeth. It was a hell of a fucking bite, begging your pardon.

'"Unbelievable, man," I told them in order to break the silence. "Just as well that you're the best of friends."

'"And what the fuck do you care?" said Menaplenty angrily, facing up to me. "Keep out of it, this is our business."

'"I don't care if they skin you alive. You're just as bad as each other... I'm off to work!"

'"Where are you going, man?" said Gobs in a friendly way, getting up and pushing away the other fella as if he now hated him again. "It's starting to rain and you're not going to have any work. Anyway, you won't make the list now... and I've got things to talk to you about..." In fact, he came towards me, grabbed me by the shoulder and started to walk with me along the middle of the highway, walking slowly, almost dropping words into my ear, just itching to say under his breath:

'"Don't leave me alone with him, 'cause I swear to you I'll do him in." Menaplenty was scrubbing with the cloth and humming away as if nothing were wrong.

'"I don't know why you need to go around in his company."

'"But can't you see that he sticks to me like glue, that I can't get rid of him?"

'"Sticks to you? You're having a laugh aren't you? Isn't it you who goes looking for him?"

Gobs thought for a moment, then added:

'"That's the fucking problem! I don't enjoy myself if he's not around... And if I hang out with him, the time comes when we have to have a fight, I mean when I have to give him a hiding, whether it's needed or not... But without him I don't enjoy myself, and that's the pickle I'm in..."

'"Get away, man!" I said laughing. "If that's the case, then he's got you over a barrel. And yes, it's a right pickle..."

'Xanciño fixed his big, blue eyes on mine. They were wide open and deep set below his reddish eyebrows, as if throwing out a cold fire all by themselves.

'"Cibrán, don't ever say that kind of thing to me again, not even in jest... Even though I love you to bits I wouldn't be able to ignore it, and you know only too well what my temper's like."

'"You're having a laugh, man! On top of everything else... Keep your nonsense for those who take it seriously, 'cause with me it goes in one ear and out the other. You know only too well that I'm as big a man as anyone, a match for anybody, so no more talk of that, and let me get to work."

'"I'm serious, Cibrán. The idea that this shit has me under his spell drives me nuts. Don't think I haven't thought about it. He's like an old woman's curse, for God's sake. But do me a favour, don't leave me alone with him. I'll pay your wages for today, I've got money. Stay with us. I'm asking you as a favour to a friend."

'The truth is my feet were hurting and I felt drained because of making up with Raxada, which was non-stop and took us almost two nights and sometimes during the day too, with me wanting her so badly and her me, and 'cause of the cold we'd stayed stuck in bed all the time...

'As well as that, I was beginning to sense that the "feeling" was coming over me, as it often starts like that, with this being drained, though it's not tiredness 'cause it has nothing to do with tiredness, and sometimes it comes over me when I get up after a good night's sleep. And besides, the day was now in fact turning dirty across the sky and it had begun to drizzle and looking like it might rain heavily, 'cause here, when it gets going... And damn it, it wasn't the time to start making gravel with that weakness coming over me, and with it raining hard, just like the other times when the rain had caught me at work, and having to put up with the annoying big straw coat they lend us there to keep out the rain, which weighs a ton when it gets soaked, and you can't even move your arms with it on...! And I told myself too, just like Xanciño had said already, that there'd be nothing done on the road works today, 'cause though the new engineer who had come from Madrid would tell us that we were already two months behind and hassled us to work on good days, as soon as a few drops of water fell he'd start to curse our country's rain and would have a go at us like a wild beast, as if it was our fault... And besides that, where would they go now at seven in the morning, which is the time when the chargehands go home...? Of course, I'd given my word and...

'"What do you think, Boar? There's no need to chew it over too much... I already told you that I'd pay your day's wages. Besides, you know that if you were to ask me a favour as a friend...!"

'"Right, let's go and have a few glasses, and then we'll see. I want to at least take my clogs off, otherwise I won't last much longer."

'So we followed the road down, with Menaplenty a few steps behind us. Towards Posío, we went into old Esquilacha's pub, where the horse dealers had stopped too. There was a good fire going in the kitchen, and the muleskinners were in there having roasted chourizos with wheat bread and young wine for breakfast. Like I've said, the "feeling" was beginning to dog me, and often comes over me when I start to do things I know I shouldn't. What's true is that I felt quite sorry for myself and sad, what with not going to work, if only to check that there wouldn't be any 'cause of the rain, and to put my mind at ease in order not to break, for my part, the promise I'd made to Raxada, as I'd been so happy even when I left the house 'cause it had been a long time since I had felt that way.

'There inside the air was warm and pleasant and full of that smell of pubs in winter, which warms your heart so much and makes all the horrible things that you carry around with you in your head vanish when you go in. It smelled too of roasted chourizos and new wine, which you could already see was quite lively just by looking at the bubbles as it swirled around as soon as it poured into the cups... Outside, the rain had come down thick and dense and the day was turning dark as if it were going back on itself. When the door was opened, the gusts of wind came in as far as the kitchen, causing a cloud of smoke to spread and making the rest of the chourizos hanging above the hearth to sway...'

'...'

'What, Sir? I'm not getting away from the story for one second... I'm telling things from the beginning, as some things happened 'cause of others and if some hadn't happened then the others wouldn't have either.'

'...'

'They're not excuses! I've got nothing to apologise about as I didn't do anything, 'cause it's not your fault if you see things happen in front of you, as much as people may blame you or want to blame you.'

'...'

'Events? They're all events, the things that happen outside you as much as those that happen inside. What happened, happened, and right now there's nothing left of what happened outside me, though inside there is. Now everything is inside me, and if I don't care for clearing out what's inside, then what happened will be like it never happened.'

'...'

'Lord preserve us! I have all the respect for you that you deserve, Sir. But I also have to say things in my own way and I can't say them any other way, no matter how much I think about it. Besides that, and as you, Sir, have pointed out to me, as hard as I try the events don't come to mind one after another, all in a row, but all together and jumbled up, as if time were jumbled up too and all the hours had been jumbled up without a chance of separating one from the other, if you like. The stuff that happened during the day, if I start to think about it, I can still manage to some extent. But what happened at night... The night is crammed with things, all close together, and it seems to me that there couldn't have been enough time for so much, as if they were several nights all together, one straight after the other, or a very long night without any day in between, or like things that fit badly together, without a before or after, but all this is making even me dizzy... On top of that, I often had the "feeling" that came over me all of a sudden, and when that happens it's as if I were free from time and everything else, as if I were both here and not here...

'So getting to the point: old Esquilacha, sensing there was a bit of money around, made us a fine omelette of potatoes, chourizos and onion, and also some fried peppers, which we ate in the kitchen at the foot of the stove, where the muleskinners were roasting young chestnuts they had brought in a bag.'

'...'

'Of course, Sir! I wouldn't expect anything else from anybody from these parts... How were we going to eat without a drink? A few drops were taken...'

'...'

'I don't know, Sir, 'cause Gobs paid for everything, but it would've been two or three jars of two or three pints for everybody, which isn't a lot we might say for three young men from this land. As it was young wine and quite tart, it went down like lemonade, almost without us feeling it... The bad thing was that Menaplenty, who might have had a cold, made sure that he asked for a pint of augardente... and we helped him out a bit with that.

'Once we'd got started, as far as I was concerned I would've happily stayed there. It was alright in the warm; eating, drinking and listening to the horse dealers' banter beside the hearth with the faggots merrily blazing away and making the chestnuts explode, while outside it rained cats and dogs. But Menaplenty was tense, with his head slumped backwards as if he were looking up at the sky, and his neck tucked between his shoulders like a hunchback. The bite mark could easily be made out on his neck, and you could see that it was bleeding, and it oozed so much blood that he would wipe it with his fingers every so often, swearing each time he did it. One of the muleteers had already asked him if the kind of bump that was forming on his nape was the pox… When we'd been there over an hour, old Esquilacha, who I'd seen talking earlier with one of the muleteers while looking towards us, took me aside to ask me to get those drunkards out of there, as by now they had put away two pints of augardente and were still asking for more, and that a pair of Civil Guard would be passing by at around nine for the relief and they often made a stop at the pub, and her house was an inn for horse dealers and market traders, all of them people of good sense and decent manners, and not a bar for the town's piss artists, and that I'd be best going back to Raxada's house or my mother's if I couldn't go on to work.

'The advice was good, but the idea of having to put my clogs on again and traipse through the mud sent a shiver through my body, on account of the bruised chilblains. I told her that, and in no time at all she called me into the house and made me take my socks off, which hurt so much that I saw the Holy Face of God himself, begging your pardon. Then she made me put my feet in a basin of hot water and garlic, and wiped the infected bits with buttercup leaves that she brought from the garden and which she scrunched up in her hands, spitting on them and then spreading pig fat on them, begging your pardon, which greatly eased the pain… When she was finishing off, and without stopping to give me advice, as she's a good friend of my mother's and a shrewd woman, the others appeared, by now quite sozzled, cracking nasty jokes because they found me sat on the bed, as if wanting to say that I was getting cosy with old Esquilacha who is old enough to be my mother.

'Our faces turned large and red like carnival masks, what with the slaps and scratches and with the drinks and the closeness of the fire. Seeing those two in such a condition, and at the very moment when I was about to decide not to leave with them, the muleskinner popped in to tell us, in a hurried voice, that a pair of Civil Guards had just come in, who were said to be on the look out for some boozers who'd been involved in a big scrap on the road. Some market women, the ones who come to town early to sell vegetables, had told them, and the men were perhaps the same ones who caused another scuffle on Saturday night in Chaguazoso's pub. I didn't believe it, 'cause you could easily see that the muleskinner fella was a right bigmouth with the matter of the market women seeing us. I was sure that nobody except them had passed by when the other two were trying to do each other in, and that it was in fact them who told the story as they were very crafty men, the ones from the border with northern León, and they had a lot of that cunning that is picked up along the world's byways too.

'But whether I was right or wrong, it was best to clear off... So we left through the orchard and began to walk under that deluge of water that showed no sign of stopping, and getting onto a path that crossed more orchards, we made our way towards Pelamios Bridge. The sky was low, leathery and dark, and the rain was hurtling down with blasts of cold wind. We continued along the banks of the Barbaña until we reached the outskirts of Burga, where we took shelter beneath the bridge. The other two, who could hardly move their legs what with the drink, wrapped themselves up in the blanket, lay down on the ground and were soon snoring like pigs, save for their blessed souls. The city seemed to have been drowned by that endless emptying of the sky, and it made your heart sad. It was already bothering me that I hadn't had more to drink, 'cause with one thing and another, the "feeling" was beginning to irritate me as if from afar, only this time it wanted to throw itself on me and plunge me into its darkness, as was always the case...

'When they woke up, about an hour later, it was still raining heavily and the day had become even gloomier, as if night were about to fall. They spoke of going here and there, but as you couldn't go anywhere in that weather and those two couldn't help playing pranks. Menaplenty got the urge to go up to the Andrada garden, which was close by, to scale the big wall to see if we could see the lady, as in town they used to say that each morning, at the first light of dawn, she went out to the gallery that looked onto the garden to give crumbs to the birds which, it seems, came to eat from her hand, all cheeping loudly, and it's even said they seemed to be talking to her.

'I'd heard the tale just like everybody else: that story of Don Fernando de Andrada and his wife, and I'd given it the same time of day as all the other loads of gossip that comes and goes from one person to another in this town of layabouts. As it rains here seven months of the year, people entertain themselves by rabbiting on, sat round tables and braziers, or in the inns and cafés, dwelling upon such fantasies.

'As far as could be seen, and according to rumours that had been brewing for years and that I'd been hearing since I was a boy, the heir of the Andradas, who was the only living member of a family killed off by a bout of consumption which struck them hard, and which had gradually taken them one by one, had spent all his youth abroad where they'd sent him so that the illness wouldn't get him. They told incredible things about him, just as poor people often do when talking about the rich, which in the end might not amount to so much... That there had been episodes of gambling and love affairs; that he'd been in a war somewhere out there among people who have nothing to do with us; that he'd secretly been a friend of a queen 'cause they say he was as fine and strapping a lad as anyone had ever known; that he really did know how to speak all the languages of the world and such and what have you... I think it's all just the chit chat of gossipy women, tailors and seamstresses who have this habit of being loose with their tongue and going around nosing about other people's reputations... What seems to have been true is that he'd returned, by now quite exhausted from his travels the world over, to take charge of his inheritance, which is said to have still been considerable. Rumour has it he didn't discuss the matter of the inheritance with anyone, and it was all sorted out by some lawyers working together to snatch from the grasp of the San Francisco friars a good part of the pie they'd nabbed from the mother, who had died insane so they say, but that's nothing to do with me. So it's said he travelled once again through those godforsaken lands, and after all those years he came back again, bringing with him a lady of such beauty that the few who'd seen her would say they'd never seen anything like her... But nobody saw her again from the day they returned, some twelve years ago now, which was when I heard them tell the story. It seems that Andrada put his wife in the house, closed the doors and dealt with not a single living soul, nor was he ever seen going around town, not even when the King came, nor when the Feirreiría quarter burnt down, even when the fire was about to lick the walls of the house on the side nearest the city... Sometimes they say he was seen on horseback at dawn, but off the roads, near a farm he owns with another big house around Santa Cruz de Arrabaldo way, and other times too at night, which made people very afraid... There was a lot of talking for talk's sake, but nobody could say what he looked like nor how he was dressed, and it all had to be idle chit-chat and old wives' tales... They also say that the servants he brought from those lands where he'd been didn't speak like us and that he changed them from year to year, or before that if he saw them talking to someone from the town, but I never knew of anybody that had spoken to them, and that's the way with stories and the accounts made up by people with enough time on their hands to give their godforsaken tongues something to do... And it was also said that he would travel every so often and nobody knew where he was going, and that he took everybody with him, except the lady who was never heard of again... Some said he had her locked away 'cause he was jealous of even the air that touched her, and that she'd been unfaithful to him with a friend in those faraway lands, and that he'd brought her by force to have her stuck in that house for the rest of her life, as if it was a prison. Others said that being treated that way had sent her mad, and it's even said that he paid her when he was with her in the matrimonial way, as if she were a whore, while others swear that he'd killed her and buried her in the garden... It's amazing how much people think about things that have nothing to do with them, as my mother says, and it was her who told me the greater part of all this.

'So the three of us and each one told what he knew, which was like whistling in the dark and pissing in the wind, but as we didn't know where to go, or couldn't go anywhere, we had to talk about something. But Menaplenty kept on about wanting to see her. And Gobs, who from the start didn't seem at all interested in what we were talking about (even though he put his pennyworth in too), just stood there still and sullen, when Menaplenty blurted out all of a sudden:

'"Well that stuff about him killing her isn't true... It isn't true, 'cause I saw her with my very own eyes two years ago, more or less..."

'"A likely story, sunshine...! You dreamt it, or you saw her one day when you got even more blotto than usual," I said, not just 'cause I didn't believe him but so that the other fella, who was as stubborn as a mule, didn't start wanting to follow Menaplenty on his mad escapade, as I knew only too well that he wouldn't dare to all by himself.

'"I'm telling you I saw her, just as I can see you both now…! Me and Bobbin saw her…"

'"…and if not, we'll go and ask him in the graveyard."

'"You could call witnesses closer to hand!"

'"We went up there one day at dawn, crawling up the ivy on the great wall. We'd been on a bender the night before, but we weren't drunk any more like we are now, 'cause I sober up quickly, as you well know… It was a split second, 'cause I couldn't hold on for long as I'm not very strong, and besides that I'd scraped my hands crawling up. And as for Bobbin, well, you already know what he was like, the poor bugger, and I don't know how he managed to get up to the edge. We saw her for a split second and we were amazed at such a thing, so much so that I didn't even want to tell anybody… They say that others also managed to climb up on occasion, but when head they popped their nut over the top of the wall, over there, see, where the summerhouse is, they were forced down with a few rounds of salt cartridges fired from the gallery of the big house. One was Dregsdrinker and the other was Rodeiro, who they told me works in the foundry."

'"I don't know if it's true," interrupted Gobs, looking all serious, "but I heard the same one day from Bobbin too… I didn't believe him, 'cause he was quite the storyteller when he started to talk about women, and they say that's why he went down with the illness that got a hold of him, 'cause he was so consumed with thinking about them so much, and that morning, noon and night he did nothing else. And I also heard from him that she was the most beautiful woman he'd seen or dreamt of, and that ever since he'd seen her he found it hard to get to sleep for a long, long time."

'"That happens a lot to those who've got tuberculosis, and a cousin of mine who died from consumption had problems sleeping…"

'"Well this subject's beginning to get on my nerves now," said Gobs with that hard look he got whenever he made a decision. "I reckon we should climb up there… What else are we going to do here?"

'"I don't know if I'll be able to, what with the bite this animal sank into me; it's starting to hurt my neck so much that I can't even move it… But I'll come with you and tell you what you have to do. And maybe I can climb up too."

'"What do you say?" Gobs asked me. After thinking about it for a second, I said:

'"It's mad if you ask me. And with this rain… As far as I'm concerned, you both know I'm not afraid… But I'll tell you straight that I don't believe in these old wives' and madmen's tales… Now, if you want… Of course, I'm not going to be able to with these clogs and this itching and pain in my feet… But since we've got into this business I'll go with you, just like a friend should."

'The objections I made to his decision were the truth and had foundation. My feet felt as if they'd been skinned and hurt me right to the top of my shins. But when you're with friends you have to do what the others do, or part company with them.

'So we came out from under the bridge and after quickly crossing the open ground which is there, went into the alley that runs along the side of the wall of the Andradas' garden. I glanced up and saw that not even a monkey could climb up there.

'"Damn and blast!" murmured Menaplenty. "He made them cut the ivy and put lime on the crack in the wall… When we came here it wasn't like this. Let's go around and see if there's another place to climb up."

'We went round the big wall, which changes direction at that point, and after walking a bit we saw, almost covered by a pile of earthworks, a big hole in the ground, and which went right through the wall's foundations, as if somebody had been making a mine. There was no one at work there, 'cause of the rain, no doubt. After thinking for a second about what it might be, we realised that it was where the waters from the new ditch were meant to run through, just like they were doing in a lot of other houses, 'cause they say now that rich people are going to have running water in their houses, but I'll believe it when I see it… So even though we were going to get filthy in the mud, 'cause the place was swimming in it, we went through the hole, and after a few steps saw the sky above us and the branches of some trees through another hole that rose up vertically above us.

'"Get over here," ordered Gobs in that way he had of ordering people around when he was in that mood, and wouldn't take no for an answer. I crouched down a little, and after throwing the blanket over my back, he got onto my shoulders until he could reach the bit above the hole resting on his elbows. He kept an eye out for a while and then leapt down; he was slightly dazed, and leaned against the wall of the tunnel with his eyes fixed on us.

'"There she is!" he blurted out, all shaken up.

'"Who, man?"

'"The woman, that lady…"

'"Didn't I tell you?" pretended Menaplenty, acting as if he were sad that it was true. "But did you see the look of her?"

'"Jesus, she looks like nothing from this world! I'm dumbstruck…"

'"Stop pissing around… I'm twenty-four and I don't believe in fairies anymore."

'"…Jesus!" He kept talking, as if he hadn't heard us. "Move over there, let me take another look at her."

'"In that case, I want to see what this is all about…"

'Aladio took out a bottle of augardente that he'd stolen in the inn and brought along in the pocket of his sheepskin jacket, and we swigged a few good mouthfuls to pep us up a bit. Then we grabbed some planks that were lying there and began to skewer them, like supports, into the soft earth of the tunnel wall, until we had made something like rungs in a ladder. I took off my clogs, tied them together to hang them around my neck and climbed up first. The hole looked out upon a small grove of camellias, so dark that the flowers looked like tiny coloured lights. At that moment I was afraid. Not of anything in this world, 'cause I'm not one to run away from the things that this world brings, although that's not so much the case with something that could come from God knows where. The large drops of the heavy, thundery rain drummed down on the leaves of the camellias. I didn't want to go up until the others had arrived, and I even felt like getting down from there without seeing anything. But then they turned up and fell down beside me.

'"So?" I grunted under my breath, elbowing Gobs.

'"Look over there," and he gestured towards a small door that was in a clump of bushes.

'And that's just what we did… Up there in the gallery, where one of the windows was open, could be seen the most beautiful woman I have ever set eyes on, even in a painting. She shone like the Blessed Virgin in the heavens, begging your pardon. She was white, so white, with black hair… Her arms were naked, full of jewels, reaching out of the window as if she wanted them to get wet in the rain, and she had an outfit on, white too, and light for the weather, as if the cold didn't bother her one bit. And she had a shawl or a blue veil around half her head, and its ends fluttered out of the window in the wind, and 'cause the lady was so still, they seemed to be the only thing that was real. She was smiling, gazing over to where we were, but without blinking, with her dark eyes, large and wide open, which were frightening in their own way...

'Then, across the misty windows, the shape of a man could be seen through the gallery, and we crouched down again without looking away. Shortly afterwards a tall, very thin gentleman with a long red beard, covered in a straw cape just like a priest or friar to protect him from the rain, came to the window and stood next to the lady. He was smoking a long cigar and his eyes were restless, glaring like a madman's. He cast an eye over the garden and started to babble in a language we couldn't understand, and when he lowered his voice his lips didn't stop moving, whether he was speaking or not... He placed a hand on the beautiful lady's head and gestured with his beard towards the garden as if he were trying to show her something, blurting out endless, hateful words all the while, though the beautiful lady said nothing back to him, nor did she stop smiling... Then he went and grabbed her firmly, clutching her by the shoulder, and pushed her backwards with a slap, without her falling over; it was as if the lady were sat on something with wheels. Then he appeared again, talking at full tilt, then shouting, and started to tear at the hairs of his beard, blowing them off the palm of his hand, puffing strongly... And with that he let out a tremendous roar of laughter, stuck two fingers up towards the sky and lowered the window with such a strong shove that I don't know how the glass didn't break to smithereens.

'All of that startled me so much I found myself at the bottom of the hole without hardly using the plank rungs, with my arse in the mud and shaking all over as if I were having a fit. The others got down in much the same way, and the three of us were sweating as if we were inside an oven. And without saying a word, we got up, took another good swig from the bottle, and when we were ready to clear off a shotgun blast was heard and bits of the camellia leaves fell on us...'

'...'

'Yes, Sir, all that is true and everything happened just as I've said. I swear to you on the memory of my late father...'

'...'

'No, Sir, I've no appetite to eat anything, nor am I tired. And besides, talking about all this has relieved me of the "feeling", which fucked me up, begging your pardon, all the time you had me in the cells of the police station, and it didn't even give me a chance to think about what had happened.'

'...'

'As Sir wishes, as long as you let me wait here, which is something I'd be very grateful to you for. If they take me back to the station, I don't know what'll happen... I'd rather them take me to gaol once and for all. Nobody can lay a hand on the face of a young healthy man with his hands bound by cuffs without him wanting to die right there and then... That isn't what real men do and I don't know how Christian men can do that to other Christian men. So I'm begging you kindly to...'

'...'

'God bless you, Sir. God bless you alright... And just as you wish, Sir... And I'll be seeing you, God willing...'

CHAPTER TWO

'…'

'But why, Sir?'

  '…'

  'In solitary confinement? And what's all that about?'

  '…'

'If that's the way it is, then that's the way it has to be, since it's you who says so. But what harm would it do anyone if she gave me the food that she's brought with her?'

  '…'

'If that's the way it is, then what can the poor old lady do? She's here now, anyway… Just to give her a hug and comfort her so she knows I didn't do anything bad and that I'm here to give a statement, and that nobody can accuse me of something I didn't do… Besides, I want to know how Raxada and the little one are getting along. I think a man has the right to know how his family are.'

  '…'

'No, Sir, she's so deaf that I'll be damned if you couldn't hear what I'm saying to her without moving an inch from here. And maybe we won't even talk at all once I've asked her about Raxada and the little one. The poor old girl grew tired of speaking to me years ago, and I regret the day she tossed me out into the world, 'cause it would have been better if she'd tossed me into the pig sty, begging your pardon! She doesn't speak to me any more. She looks at me with those silent tears which have driven furrows into her wrinkles, like someone who looks at somebody else who is beyond help, and it would've been better if she'd buried me with curses. Now she just tells me: settle down, my son, settle down… When are you going to settle down once and for all, my boy?'

'…'

'Right, just as you say Sir, 'cause I understand nothing of the law, nor do I need to… but I hope she finds her reward in Heaven.'

'…'

'Nothing, Sir, nothing. I was talking to myself. Sorry.'

'…'

'Yes, Sir… Well, as I was saying…, it kept bucketing down…'

'…'

'Well Sir, it might seem that way to you…! But I'm telling you the rain was very much to blame… If it weren't for that rain spitting down on me when I went off after being with Raxada, and that heavy rain that fell mercilessly and which later washed over the whole world so much that it was like walking through a nightmare with no chance of escape, many things that happened wouldn't have happened, as I would have gone to work without a care in the world. My word is my bond… 'Cause it's one thing what you do with your daily wage, and something very different being a lazy sod and not able to cope with life, or wanting to go through it acting like a fool. I'm a hardworking man, everybody knows that, and I'm never off work except for when there is none. And I like it in summer and winter, come rain or shine, and I'd go so far to say that even on these cold winter days I enjoy getting stuck into the job. You wouldn't know, Sir, and you have no reason to, 'cause you're an educated man. But I'm telling you that turning up there half crippled, throwing off your jacket, spitting on your hands and starting to smash the stones to make gravel, until you feel your blood beginning to boil and the urge to belt out a song rising up through your throat… And as for the sun when it breaks out over the hills... Well, it's all fucked up now anyway!

'So, as I was saying, we stopped by the large spout of the Burga fountain. We made kindling for a fire out of a wooden box we found there, so that we could dry ourselves off and roast a bit of sausage meat that Menaplenty had grabbed in old Esquilacha's inn, 'cause that fella, well...

'They polished off the leftover augardente, and when they had finished eating they had yet another kip, and I don't know how some people manage to nap whenever they feel like it... I began to think, and to think, just as I often do when I don't have the "feeling". 'Cause the "feeling" is something quite different to thinking. When I think, I'm in charge, but when the "feeling" comes over me, I become somebody else, just as if I weren't myself any more... I thought about Raxada, who would have gone by now, in all that godforsaken rain, to bring me my lunch at the road works just as we'd arranged, just as she always did, just as happy and smiling when we were alright, and in good weather she would bring the boy too and we'd meet up there, at the foot of some strawberry trees... And I also thought about what my father, who I didn't know, would have been like, although what they used to say about him it was no great loss. And I thought about my brother who'd vanished without a trace and who never came back from his travels, and my little sister, and those illnesses she got and that way of hers of lying pale and still for hours on end. It would've been better if God had taken her, 'cause they say it all came from the sickness that my father brought back when he'd been a roadsweeper in Cadiz as a young man... And then I thought about other things, about things that had already happened and those which had yet to happen, 'cause this is the trouble I have, thinking, not just about what happened but also about what can happen, 'cause I see that just like it'd already happened... If I didn't think, I said to myself, I would be like all those fellows there, dirty buggers, knocking their heads together with their guts full of food and drink, snoozing like children between one mad turn and another. But the damned trouble is that I go from thinking about things that are real to things that aren't, and with one thing and another I always get on to death, and then I don't think any more, 'cause when I reach that moment the "feeling" comes over me, which isn't like things going through your head one by one with their names, with their faces... The "feeling" is like thinking of everything all at once, with all my body, and everything comes to me so confused and dreadful that if it lasted for a long time I'd have no choice but to die... When it comes over me very strongly, it's as if something were growing inside me which isn't me, and as if my wrists were about to explode, and my chest swells up so much that it's as if it was going to burst into smithereens... But at other times it comes over me very gently, warmly, like when you're tired and go to sleep and begin to sink down, down... Which is when it scares me the most, and sometimes I wake up all of a sudden, 'cause I've thought that this very gentle sinking feeling can have no other end but death... And maybe it's death that's coming after me to take me away without me getting sick, like someone who's sleeping... I often take to the wine to get rid of that, although I don't go on a bender. Wine is the only thing that rids me of the "feeling", and takes away the bitterness from this sense of sinking down inside which can only end in death... I don't know if you understand me, Sir, but now you know.'

'...'

'I was getting to that, Sir, but I couldn't if I didn't get out what I've already said, which has to help us understand each other concerning other things that I'm meaning to say...

'So that cold, blustery rain, which made the steam thicker as it rose up out of the hot water from the big washing place of the Burga, kept on falling and the air was thick with the stench of cloths and soap, and also with the shit that, begging your pardon, the women removed when cleaning out the tripe in the lower basin, where the chickens and hens were plucked too. There they were, the poor devils, their heads covered with shawls, stuck between the cold rain and the boiling water, with their long hair making the rain run down their necks, cleaning the chickens for the masters. Poor sods! And some of them were even singing. "The damned life of the working man" as Serantes says…

'When those swines woke up, I wanted to convince them that it would be best for each of us to clear off home. But they didn't want to. To tell you the truth, I wasn't very keen on it either. We talked about what we'd do, and I said we should to go and eat at an inn. They looked at each other with a certain air of mystery, but I don't know what that was all about… And it was then that Menaplenty said he knew where we could go and spend a good old afternoon, in the warmth and with good drink, only that we couldn't go empty handed and that if we gave him money he'd go to the market to look for some food to have lunch. Gobs, who was acting very flash, gave him some, and with that Menaplenty threw the blanket over his head and went into the rain, rolling up his trousers and doing funny little jumps, with that way he has of walking like a partridge.

'He didn't take long to come back with a bundle full of things… Gobs must have known by now where we were headed, 'cause he didn't ask him anything when we began to walk towards the stepping stones of the river. Along the way Menaplenty kept telling me that we were going to a relation of his who was a distiller working on the preparation of the augardente for the masters in the castle, and that we'd have a damn good time in that cellar, beside the fire, drinking as much as we wanted of that augardente which was distilling away. Even though I grunted in protest that it was very far and that we'd be soaked to the skin when we got there, the truth was that the day was made for staying under cover, no matter how hard it was for us to get there, though it was clear that those fellas, without me knowing why, were avoiding going into town at all costs, or at least going to places where we would often go on a binge, as if they didn't want to be spotted by people who knew them.

'We had to cross the Barbaña very slowly, as it was swollen after the downpour. The stepping stones were almost at the same level as the torrent, but Pelamios Bridge was still a way off. We got onto the road, taking a short cut uphill through Saltodocán. My feet hurt so badly that I ended up taking the bloody clogs off. The others sped off in front of me, covered with the blanket, without letting me rest. From time to time they let out a wail, or burst out laughing or swore when their feet knocked against the stones of the track.

'As we continued to climb, the rain grew harder and more ferocious with gusts from the northeast. It hit my body as if it were raining sideways, lashed my face till it hurt and got under my clothes, making my body wet, as if I was actually wearing it. The farmland was sodden, with the ditches almost flooded, and when we took a short cut across the lower ground, our feet sank up to our calves.

'In the end we reached the chestnut grove on the hill, where the manor house that belongs to the masters of the castle was, and we stopped at the edge of the field to take a breath, stuck to the outside wall at the foot of a cypress grove, which didn't offer a lot of bloody cover. We were so drenched that it was impossible to roll a cigarette. The packets of cigarette paper had become a lump, their gum all stuck together, and the rain had even got into our cigarette cases. I began to feel shivery and I wasn't sure if it was pain, hunger or fever, and I felt the sting of my chilblains, as if my feet were being scratched by glass.

'"What's happening here?" then Xanciño Gobs said, shaking his jacket.

'"I haven't told my relative to expect us," said Menaplenty. "But it doesn't matter. Come with me." We walked a few steps and went through the orchard gate.

'"Hole up in that hut while I go and talk to him."

'We went in very slowly, going behind some carts so they wouldn't see us from the house, which was on the other side of a yard, fairly large like a square, with sheds all around the edges full of farm tools. You could see it was a well-off house. On the bannisters of the passages, wooden balconies and galleries that looked onto the yard, the ears of corn, shining with the rain, hung all tangled together and thick, like one continuous yellow curtain.

'Not long after this, Menaplenty gestured to us from a doorway and we went over to him. His relative was waiting for us behind the door, his face the image of carefree mischievousness. He was red from being close to the fire and his eyes were merry and tipsy. As soon as he began to speak I realised that he was an acquaintance of mine called Magpie, who I hadn't seen in a long time. He wasn't from town, but we'd hung out together at the Santiago de Caldas and Santa Ana fairs: it would be three or four years ago now.

'He was one of those lads from the Gustei plateau who like a good time, and who tend to hang out singing and drinking in the streets or at house gathering for most of the winter and from one fair to another all summer. He had lived in the town as a young boy learning a trade, I don't know which one, and all that he'd learned had been scams and swindles from Auria's finest low lifes, 'cause village folk, once they get going , end up even more lively than we are... When he reminded me how he knew me, I also remembered that we'd seen each other again in Tui when I was in the King's service. He was going about with a knife-sharpening wheel and a deck of cards, among cattle traders, hucksters, castrators and pickpockets, all from Moura or roundabouts, and all good people, who moved from one trade to another according to circumstance, bright as buttons, oh yes, and who went on the hunt for the many Portuguese who would come to Tui for the town fiestas. He also told me that as he was now almost twenty five, he had settled down and was behaving himself more, as his father was crippled now, and he had to handle the running of the augardente still, which was a serious trade.

'You could see that the wine cellar belonged to a rich and wealthy house, where there was all kind of food and drink: chourizos, hams, big whole hunks of salted pork hanging from the ceiling; I don't know why Menaplenty bothered to bring anything with him, unless it was as a gesture... Next to the walls there were some big barrels which were so tall they almost touched the beams in the ceiling.

'So Magpie fetched and began to give us some of that newly-made augardente in some little white cups, the ones they use for young wine, and it was like a gift from God, feeling it drip warmly down the gullet just like a sweet and warm syrup, and it was like hardly feeling it at all.

'Gobs, ever since we'd arrived, had been quiet and thoughtful without taking part in what was talked about, without even saying thank you or paying any compliment about the drink. He would top up on augardente without saying a word, just holding the little cup out to the distiller, as if the drink had to be paid for and they were obliged to give it to him, and the way he carried on even made me feel ashamed. All morning he'd had these moments of uneasy silence, so you couldn't even ask him what the matter was, 'cause even though he was quite gruff by nature, when we were on a bender he would prove to be a bit of a reveller and quite the joker, and those moods didn't last long.

'With the third cup that he emptied almost without catching his breath, his face turned red and his eyes shone blue-green, quite sincere and pretty like those of a child, though somewhat darkened by the eyelashes which he often scrunched together, squinting as if he couldn't see well, and his eyebrows were quite thick and dark... So, as if waking up from a dream, he turned towards me and said, as if he were following a conversation already in flow:

'"...well, I'll tell you again that she was a hell of a woman... I can't stop thinking about it, for fuck's sake! What do you reckon, Boar?"

'Menaplenty, who was fiddling around, kept quiet while the other fella spoke, but then, as if to avoid the subject and talking to the distiller, he said:

'"And won't anybody come round here who might give you bother?"

'"You can be at your leisure and relax... There's no-one with any authority in the manor and we have the house to ourselves until tonight... The masters are in the city 'cause of the lady's mother who's very poorly: they even say she won't survive the next few days. And Mr Marcial left quite early on horseback going Piñor way, to see about some rents..."

'"And who's Mr Marcial?"

'"The Grasshopper, or the steward. He's got a bigger temper than the devil who made him!"

'"And the other people in the house?"

'"Well, in this weather, and without Grasshopper here, they're stuck around the fire, drinking and munching away, 'cause here nobody keeps tabs on them. Only in a well-off house like this...! What they can't do, though, is go into the wine cellar. They've caused all kinds of aggro! My father told me, so I'd be on my guard, that one Christmas Eve when the masters went to town to be with their relatives, they raised the kind of hell that blows the roof off... After eating their fill like the swine they are, save for their blessed souls, and drinking until they threw up, they were possessed and they decked themselves out from head to toe in the masters' clothes. They tucked into frock coats and bustles and went off to dance the ribeiranas in the mirror room with Fuca and Cabbage, who are the oldest servants, sitting up on the stage acting like lords, and who by the looks of it were as drunk as two of those mad old boys that crop up in those boozy fiestas that go back to old Auria, and they say the day after they couldn't remember a thing. When the masters got back mid-morning, seems like there was a great rumpus, and many were still sleeping it off wherever sleep had got the better of them, even when that was in the masters' and the children's beds, which it seems was what caused the most anger... And even though the masters are as good as gold, they threw everybody out except the old folk. There was nobody left of the younger servants, even though they apologised and tried everything they could... And they even say that two girls from Rairo, who were paid by the day for needlework, ended up pregnant after that, though people do talk a lot... But the fact is that since that time nobody can go into the wine cellar without permission, much less when the distiller is around, 'cause it seems that back then, when they hung around the still with the aim of having a taste of the augardente, they would get plastered so often that..."

'Magpie was quite the chatterbox, and when he started nattering he would rattle on without stopping even for a quick rest. I wasn't minded to talk back, and as far as I could see the others let him blather on too without giving much credence to what he was saying.

'Gobs was hunched up beside the fire, next to me. We were very tired and our clothes were stuck to us like a skin that was gradually shrinking, and it made our bodies itch. Menaplenty was buzzing about as usual, humming away, and talking about getting lunch ready, 'cause he always had to be doing something. When he emptied the knapsack he'd used to carry his things, some coins rolled out, eight or ten of them, from behind the cover of the kneading trough where he was pottering about, and he went all red.

'"Where did you get that money from?" asked Gobs, raising an eyebrow.

'"Oh, I don't know!" replied Menaplenty, his voice soft and gentle and full of falseness. "They must have fallen out from Delfina's knapsack when I bought the ham off her, I swear to God, 'cause she's very absent minded. What a pity, poor girl! What'll she be like when she realises they're gone!" And with that he let out that giggle through his nose. The others laughed too, cottoning on to the swindle. But I didn't laugh, 'cause we are what we are, but swindlers have never made me laugh, as it's one thing to be a piss artist and quite another to be a thief, though some do it on purpose only to pretend they'd made a mistake or blame it on being drunk or going on a booze up, even though they're not on one at that moment: the things that come out of the poison in their souls...

'I was shivering for a good while, as if a cold were coming over me, and it was then that Menaplenty said to me:

'"Take your clothes off and put them to dry. If you keep them on you'll catch pneumonia with the soaking that you've had." And as he was saying this he started to pull at Gobs' jacket, but he threw him off with a shove.

'"He's dead right," added Magpie. '"You can relax at your pleasure like I've told you, 'cause nobody's coming in here."

'Shortly after that Gobs began to undress, until he was down to his underpants. Then he let them fall too and started to untie the laces of his high shoes and in the end he was naked as the day he was born.

'"And you're going to strip off too," he said in a menacing voice to Menaplenty, while he threw his clothes haphazardly upon the back of the still. His body was white and firm, his mossy flesh stuck to his bones, and seemed much stronger than when he was dressed. On his chest a shallow wound could be seen, like a gash, which went towards his shoulder. He began to scratch the scab with the edge of his fingernail; you could see that it was a fresh wound, until it started to bleed again. Then he grabbed a little ash and dressed it with it, putting it through the lips of the wound, and to see him do that without blinking, like he was burrowing into somebody else's flesh, sent shivers down your spine.

'"How did you get that, man?" I asked him.

'"That's his larking around," put in Menaplenty. "He likes to get stuck in, and that's what you get..."

'"Are you going to shut your trap, you little shite?" shouted Gobs, moving towards him.

The other fella ran over behind a barrel to take cover, and Xanciño said for our benefit:

'"It was nothing... I had a few words with Balbino Onions and he took out a knife. A knife for me! He got something for his troubles... I'm all for bare hands, but I can't stand a steel blade before my eyes... I can't help myself..."

'Magpie listened without looking at him, and then asked him, in a worried voice, making it sound as if he was all concerned:

'"Was it last night in Chaguazoso's pub?"

'"Yes, why?" replied Gobs, staring at him suspiciously.

'Magpie didn't answer, though the other fella asked him again, 'cause he saw that he'd left something unsaid. Then he started to talk about when the rain would ease off, about what we were going to do about leaving, as it wouldn't be convenient if night came on us there, and things like that, getting away from the point, which proved that he was uncomfortable about us being there, after what Xan had said.

'I could feel my damned clothing stuck so tight to my body that it was itching like it was infested with lice. And in the end, as we were among men, I too ended up stripping off and putting my clothes by the fire. It was then that Menaplenty came back, half naked too. With that way he had of doing everything, he grabbed a thick rope and started to hang out everyone's clothing, stretching it out properly. From his waist down he'd made an apron out of a few dishcloths, which covered him across the front and left his large buttocks uncovered, shaking and full of blotches like a child's. His skin was whitish and full of bruises from the knocks he had taken, and his flabby flesh extended down his sides and his back as if he were made of butter and didn't have tendons to hold the flesh up like other men. On his chest, without a wisp of hair, his nipples wobbled when he moved, for God's sake, like he was a woman. Magpie suddenly had a fit of laughter when he saw him like that, and I thought that he was choking, so as he passed by I gave him a slap on his arse that exploded like a firework.

'"Oh, fuck off!" yelled Menaplenty. "Keep your hands to yourselves, right! And you, see if you can stop laughing as this is no fancy dress." And with that he continued to fiddle about with the preparations for lunch, humming through his nose and swinging his hips as he walked, something that you no longer knew whether to laugh at or be sickened by.

'Gobs, after walking up and down stretching for a bit, squatted down next to me again and stayed there with his gaze fixed on the fire for a good while, without blinking.

'"And what's up with you, man, looking all serious? That's not your normal mood when you're on a bender. Something's up..."

'"That woman's something else," he muttered in a low voice as if talking to himself. Menaplenty's ear was cast upwards trying to catch what we were chatting about.

'"Well I can't get it out of my head either. She really is something else..."

'"What a load of old crap!" interrupted Menaplenty. "For God's sake! So the spells in old wives' tales really do work." And with that he continued to beat some eggs in a bowl.

'"What woman are you talking about, if you don't mind my asking?" said Magpie. The three of us looked at each other and made no reply, as if we'd agreed to keep a secret. The other fella asked us again and Menaplenty replied, without making too much of it:

'"Well blow me! The things people say when they've had too much dodgy wine! When they get leathered they think that everything they saw was true. Don't pay them any attention... Where do you keep the onions?"

'The rain kept coming down and the deluge could be heard rushing down from the heights of the chestnut grove, smashing against the vines of the orchard and pouring along the paths that had been turned into streams. I daubed my feet in the ash to get rid of that mixture of pain and itching that I couldn't stomach, and I was even more bewildered. It still looked as if there was going to be a thunderstorm, though from the north this time. It had grown so dark we had to light an oil lamp, and it seemed as if night had already fallen. How comfy it was there! In that gentle warmth beside the fire, with that lovely augardente I was drinking slowly so that I could enjoy it with a clear head, while outside the wind howled against the corners of the big house and tore the branches from some bushes that could be seen through the window that looked onto the manor's gardens... If it hadn't been for the smell of the food Menaplenty was cooking, I would've even enjoyed falling asleep just as I was, naked, with my forehead resting against my knees, hearing the bundles of kindling whistle in the still's fire, free from the "feeling"...

'We ate like lords and drank our fill from the best of the old harvest that Magpie kept bringing in a milking pail from a barrel which belonged to the masters. We must have emptied a good half dozen pails, almost without feeling it, and not only 'cause we ate a great deal, but 'cause it went down well too, gentle and coarse at the same time, and it wasn't like that young, weak wine that you drink like water and never get drunk on. Then we went back on the augardente, though this time it was flambéed with dark sugar... By God, how comfy we were, in the gentle warmth of that fat wine cellar, so much so that it was hard to think that it would soon come to an end and that you'd have to put up once again with the rain, the wind and everything else in this bastard world...!

'While I was thinking, the others sang, danced and raised the roof, doing all the mad things that came into their heads. Menaplenty threw on a few strings of garlic, as if they were necklaces, and mimicked a saucy café singer, shaking his hips just like a whore, begging your pardon. Magpie and Gobs did a few slow dances with him, and every time Gobs stole his dancing partner from the other fella, he did it so badly that it was like he was goading him into a fight. I didn't want to get involved because I hated men behaving like that with each other. Menaplenty was taking the piss out of me, calling me a baby, and even tried to burn me somewhere I shouldn't say with a stick that he grabbed from the fire, and I put up with everything he did until he went and said:

'"Look what the poor bastard has got there, it looks like the one on Shabby's donkey! I don't know how Raxada copes with it..." It was then I lost my temper and hit him so angrily I almost knocked him into the fire, hardly noticing the wallops the others were giving me to make me let him go. All the while, Menaplenty was squealing like a pig on the killing block, but you couldn't tell if his yells were enjoyment or complaint 'cause they were like screeches as much as laughter, and this was what wound me up the most, so I was giving him everything I could, 'cause I'm not one to hold back when they start to hit... That was when they pulled me off, 'cause I was furious and wanted to keep on giving him a whipping. Magpie threw me on top of a pail full of wine to calm me down, and it did. But then Gobs wanted to fight me and I was up for it too. So as soon as we grabbed each other, Magpie began to swear at the top of his voice, brandishing a stake at me. Menaplenty was squealing loud enough to split your eardrums, and with our bodies so softened up by the drink we kept hitting one another, and began to throw things at each other, anything that came to hand: plates, pots of food, glasses... So as Gobs threw a stool at me, I went and whacked him with the oil lamp, but such was my luck that it ended up smashing against the wall and setting fire to some bundles of straw and wood that were there to feed the still. The fire spread quickly, and when we were trying to put it out, a boy popped his head through the window and said:

'"The Grasshopper's here!" And with that we went through the courtyard shouting "Fire! Fire! Fire!"

'We grabbed our clothes as best as we could, and still hadn't put our trousers on when a gentleman in gaiters with a rod in his hand appeared in the doorway. We retreated and left by the lower window that looked out onto the road. Just like that, half naked as we were, we sneaked up the side of the hill and we didn't stop until the chestnut grove, where we finished pulling our clothes on, going down almost head over heel until we hit the new road. There we got our breath back, resting a little while. Then, making a detour, we stopped for a rest on the outskirts of Posío Park, near Burga Bridge. After passing along the low stone wall, we found a crowd of people looking into the distance. It had suddenly stopped raining and a wind came in from the north that swept everything away. One of the people who was walking past was saying:

'"The Castle Manor has caught fire… It's burning like dry tinder!"

CHAPTER THREE

'...'

'No, Sir, no. I'm no more or less keen to speak today than I was yesterday... The thing is that now I have to chew over things properly before saying them. I was chewing over them the whole night long as I hardly slept a damn wink, but the cursed things got all twisted together in a circle, overlapping in my brain one on top of the other, and now I don't even know which came first and which afterwards, and it seems even to me that so many things couldn't have happened in a single night like they do when you dream, as they seem never-ending and happen in a second... 'Cause I'm telling you that what happened that night is as if it happened over a load of different nights all stuck together and without any day between them, or just like I said before... So I don't know how to begin.'

'...'

'That's fine, yes, Sir... Well, what happened was that we were stupefied from tiredness and drink and didn't know where to go, as things were going from bad to worse, and we were frightened to go anywhere where there were people we knew, and they knew us in all the places where we wanted to go...

'The weather had turned cold again. On the outskirts of town not a living soul could be seen...

'The wattle and daub houses looked as if they were about to be knocked flat, and gusts of wind came swirling in from the north like they do when it's going to snow, and threads of rain that still hurtled into the middle of the street from the guttering splashed back into the air.

'We looked on with envy when we saw the inns full of people as we passed through Porta da Aira, but we didn't dare go in. Gobs was the one who took greatest care that they didn't see us, racing ahead nervously and silently without telling us where he was heading. At the San Cosme fountain we took some huge gulps of water straight from the basin which made us throw up everything we had inside us within next to no time. All three of us, begging your pardon, puked like dogs, save for our blessed souls, and with this the heaviness gradually faded and we began to be as happy as young lads, without knowing why... In the distance you could see a patch of sky lit up by the fire at the manor, and each one of us would look in that direction when we thought the others wouldn't notice. But we didn't say anything, as if it had nothing to do with us... And I kept thinking that the fire had grown huge so suddenly 'cause it would've reached the woodshed at the side of the wine cellar, and I could see it all clearly when the distiller went to look for bundles of straw for the fire...

'So we found ourselves in the Feirreiría, where we stood in a doorway to work out what to do, 'cause it wasn't right to be carrying on in like that all night, and especially with the cold that was building up.

'"How much money have you got?" asked Xanciño. I didn't have hardly anything, as I'd given all my wages to Raxada.

'"I've got ten pesos, and we're going to blow the lot of them tonight," said Menaplenty smugly.

'"I've got four or five... But we've got to keep going, they're more than enough," fibbed Gobs.

'"I'm going home, to my mother's house," I replied, 'cause that was the truth, and I wasn't in the mood to keep playing pranks as we'd played enough of them already.

'"You must be mad! With the bother we've caused, the first place they'll look for you will be at Raxada's house or your mother's. Do you think they're stupid?" said Gobs. "Let's keep going, and tomorrow's another day."

'"They've nothing to accuse me of or reason to look for me. I've done nothing nor have I had any trouble with anyone."

'"And who knocked over the oil lamp that set fire to the manor?"

'"It slipped out of my hand... I didn't do it on purpose. How did I know that it was going to go off like that, as if it was a bomb? And how is it my fault if the wood shed was so close? For fuck's sake...!"

'We argued a little more about these things, but as we didn't raise our voices it was as if weren't arguing, 'cause we talked about everything in whispers so they wouldn't hear us. So after they'd told me, one after the other, that we equally up to our necks in it, we decided to go whoring, begging your pardon Sir, though Menaplenty didn't fancy that idea very much, and he set down the condition that we weren't to go to Nonó's house but to Monfortina's, and I've no idea why...

'But they didn't want to let us in at Monfortina's, as they said they had some well-off travellers from out of town who'd taken the house as their own and ordered the door to be shut at any expense so everyone could stay overnight....That was what Fat-Arse told us, with the top half-door open and the bottom one shut to give us the idea they wouldn't open up for us. And she only popped her head out to answer 'cause she recognised Xanciño's voice, and she was fond of him, as according to rumour Gobs was a man held in high esteem by the whores. Fat-Arse leaned out to natter with us for a bit.

'"Mary Mother of God, I don't know how you dare to go about like that and in this weather... Now if we didn't have these punters, who are good friends of Monfortina..."

'"What are you up to there?" murmured Mouldy behind her,

sticking out her lardy, gluttonous features and her drunkard's nose.

'"Look, what a sorry bunch of men! They're with Xanciño Gobs..."

'"Whoever they've come for, shut the door... Today's not the day for that kind of punter. Shut the door and that's the end of it," said Mouldy nastily. She was Monfortina's right-hand girl, as you well know, Sir...'

'...'

'I'm very sorry Sir, I didn't mean to offend you, but here everybody, even well-to-do folk, knows that in whorehouses, excuse me, Sir, they know everything that's going on, just as if they were well-to-do houses too, 'cause in these small towns...'

'...'

'Yes, Sir, yes. So, Gobs told her not to be so rude, and that she could say whatever she had to say without insulting people. But Mouldy, who is quite daring, stood up to him, chest thrust forward, all dark and thick-lipped like she is with her moustache, and she began to shout:

'"Clear off, you lazy sods, you wasters, or I'll come out with the door bar! What, do you think I'm not man enough for you?" And she pulled back to avoid Menaplenty scratching her.

'"Get going," said Fat-Arse less harshly. "Here come the lamplighters with the policeman."

'"And what have we got to do with the lamplighters and the policeman?" I asked her, pretending, and also to see if they had anything solid on the other two, 'cause I had my suspicion that there would be something...

'"Oh, what a bunch of idiots!" shouted Mouldy. "Shut that door, Fat-Arse! Bloody fools whoever brought them here, 'cause they're going to get us into a spot of bother! Why did you open the door, you silly cow? Get out of the way..."

'"Well now, we'll fucking come in if we want to!" blurted out Gobs, putting his elbow between the two door halves and banging into the bit below with his knees.

'"Clear off you pox-ridden faggots, or you're all going to the cells…!"

'I pushed Gobs to one side and said to Mouldy, very quietly so that the lamplighters, who were now passing quite close, wouldn't hear the shouting:

'"Don't be like that, woman… We can work this out… We're young men who are out on a bender, with good money in our pockets to spend… And if your house is full, then there's no need to start talking about policemen and the cells, 'cause we're not from out of town or pickpockets…"

'"Don't play the bloody innocent with me! I know who you are, you're Raxada's bloke… But why are you knocking about with this lot? And don't you know that this fella," she said, gesturing towards Gobs, "left a man as good as dead in Chaguazoso's inn yesterday? So you didn't know, right? Well don't make me go on…"

'Taking advantage of us being dumbstruck on hearing such a thing, they closed the door with a bang and put the bar across. It was then they began to lob bottles at us from the floor above and we saw Fermín, the old lamplighter arrive, with a great clatter of clogs on the slabs of the street, gesturing towards us with the flaming tow on top of his pike, so wrapped up in his huge straw coat that he looked like a ghost from another world. Behind him, losing his breath, came a policeman, who judging by his height must have been Sardine, who had also come running, almost bow legged, as he often does because of his bunions, and even the lads tease him for running like that.

'"Get them! Get them!" they were shouting like devils,

undoubtedly alerted by the racket from the shower of bottles, as they hadn't spotted us until then. The windows of the neighbouring houses, well accustomed to these spectacles, opened up all of a sudden, and María Mishaps, who lived in a half-collapsed hovel which shared a wall with Monfortina's, came out covered in a sheet, screeching like a swift…

'"Come quickly neighbours, they're trying to kill me…! Help! Help!" The whores used to pay her or give her food so that she'd help them with her mad cries, turning away from the door those men who were of no use to them when they got too cocky, and the damned woman did that puppet show very well.

'We left in a hurry because Fermín and Sardine were already on top of us. When we reached Pena Vixía Passage, Gobs commanded:

'"We have to split up. If they see the three of us together, they're going to twig that it's us. Everybody go their own way. We'll meet up at Nonó's house in a second. Go in by the door on Santísima Trinidade, without knocking, through the back bit which leads to the kitchen… And don't hang about…"

'That's what we did, and in no time at all we were together again… Still today I ask myself why I didn't take advantage of that moment to get away from such people… And even more so knowing what I knew by then.'

'…'

'Perhaps it's like you say, 'cause you never know yourself properly… And when things are bound to turn out a certain way…! What I thought afterwards I could've thought then, but what's true is that I didn't, may God strike me down right here where I stand. Well, now it was a case of don't cry over spilt milk. In the end, everything got fucked up…

'So they let us into Nonó's house straight away 'cause I had a good reputation and also cause Xanciño was quite a fancyman of Lola, the girl from Vigo, who acted as the right-hand girl, and they say she was very much in love with him. Vigo Lola, as you know Sir... or rather, as everyone here knows, is the best that Nonó has, and there are four or five of them, and if she didn't have that impetuousness and that little madame's way about her, she could be busy night and day, as she's one of "the persuasive ones", as Almería, the waiter who works for Mendenúñez, says. But when it takes her fancy to be kind to someone, she's handy, as well as pretty, and it has to be true what they say about her, that she's a good person, and that if she's not in Foxy's house, which as you know charges five pesetas and not one and a half pesetas like Nonó's girls, it's 'cause she doesn't want to be. Besides, they say she likes to knock it back, and not spirits like the fancy ones, but cheap plonk which she drinks a lot and gets quite plastered on, and it's even said that she has stomach rot, excuse me, Sir, and that she stinks like us men who have that bad habit.

'So from the kitchen we went into the hall where the madame often was, as she rarely went to the sitting room. They didn't receive us in the usual manner, and even Nonó didn't answer our greeting properly. Menaplenty and I arrived first and we told Vigo Lola that Xanciño would get there in a little while, which made her quite happy and she put powder on her face and dabbed perfume on top. Then, when Gobs arrived she went over to him and grabbed him in a long hug, and the surly fella acted like he wanted to get away from her, or as if he were reluctant to let himself be fussed over, 'cause the men that whores like, excuse me Sir, are often like that, as if they were being caressed against their will, which makes the girls more agitated and chase after them even more madly, which is something that I don't understand.

'Vigo Lola was looking at such a creature as if she'd never tire of the sight of him and without letting him go, as if she was afraid he might be stolen away from her, with tearful, admiring eyes, as if an angel had come down from heaven. And that beggar let his arms droop down the side of his body, like a halfwit away with the fairies, as if the matter had nothing to do with him. If it'd been me, I know what I would've fucking done...! Well, Vigo Lola used to call him "my little pimp", as she often speaks in Castilian, but not like Showdog who'd been a seamstress in Paderne and had started to speak Castrapo, which is when it all began to go wrong for her, and for others from the five-peseta houses who speak Castrapo full of Castilian touches to act all sophisticated, and like Madrid girls with the gentlemen from town. No, you could see all too easily that that was Vigo Lola's natural way of talking, and they say that it came from her being born into a rich family, and it was even whispered that she was the daughter of a colonel from Ferrol. They say the wife and children gradually got away from him as he'd taken to the gambling a lot, 'cause people don't tire of inventing things, and it could be as much the truth as it could be a fib...

'Nonó was stretched out, right by of the brazier with her legs open, and with a fag in a corner of her mouth as always. Those legs as round as the axles of cart wheels, and her face damaged by blisters, bigger than those of an average man, no matter how big he might be, ending under her chin with two or three dewlaps, pale and hairy, and which didn't seem to belong to the rest of her... She had a bowl of wine warming on the brazier, and every so often would give it a poke, pushing the udders that she had for knockers away with one hand so that they didn't block her view, and would take long swigs without stopping. After each gulp she would belch like a priest and say to herself, without changing her serious composure:

'"Good health, Nonó. May this be the scourge that kills you and may the world go fuck itself...!" She's a haughty woman.

'"How are you, my little pimp?" murmured Vigo Lola, snuggling up to Gobs, the big lump. "How fine you'd look beside me, the two of us all cosy together, and you'd not be wanting for anything... What are you up to then...?"

'"Look, Lola, you know I love you to bits, but I wouldn't be trapped for all the fish in the sea, as they say..."

'"Get away with you, you good for nothing layabout, it's been almost two weeks since I've seen you and I even sent you a dozen messages... I wonder who you've been knocking about with...!"

'Menaplenty, who was looking at them with that little smile of his which was so annoying, and which was his way of mocking people or of giving the impression that he already knew what they were going to say, ended up not paying any attention to them at all and went to squat down next to the big woman who he was mumbling things to in a low voice, things that made her laugh, while he kept prodding the embers with the poker.

'On the other side of the door you could hear the shindig that the punters were having with their girls in the sitting room, dancing to the sound of the blind man from Cudeiro's big guitar, who was belting out mazurkas in Castrapo with a hoarse voice:

If only there were handrails over the sea,
To Brazil I'd go to see you.
But since there are less than a few,
My darling I still have no means to.
Oh, if only!

'Then, making castanets and tambourines with whatever they could lay their hands on to make a noise, two of them, who must have been Jiménez and Quintela, as they often got up to this lark, could be heard putting on a zapateado with everybody laughing, eagerly keeping the beat on the bench as if it were a drum:

Oh up on your feet,
On the tips of your toes,
Be quick on your feet,
Zapateado...
Zapateado feet and toes...

'Menaplenty and Nonó were gossiping under their breath and drinking from the bowl, and when she spoke, smoke would come out between the words, just as if the smoke and her voice were the same thing, and she didn't let out a single word that wasn't wrapped up in smoke.

'Vigo Lola began to steer her friend well away from the light thrown by the lamp that hung from the ceiling, until they were sat on the straw sofa that's in a dark corner there. She began to fuss over him, kissing his neck and giving him little nibbles on his ears, but all the greedy sod did was to stay completely stretched out, staring endlessly into the distance, his hands stuffed into his belt against his belly, without giving her the slightest caress, and it was beginning to wind me up.

'Since Nonó accused us of being "pennywise punters", two bottles of sugared anisette and another two of coffee liqueur were ordered, as our stomachs were so upset that we only felt the urge for gentle and sweet things... Later on, Fani, the servant, was sent to bring a fine pot of tripe from Xenerosa's inn that we didn't even get to taste...

'It was then that Skinny appeared in the doorway that led to the bedrooms, tidying her hair, and followed by Pepe the Corporal boy, who'd been given that nickname when he was a corporal with the sappers in the service of the King. Pepe the Corporal boy, though he was the son of Mr Argimiro the Pest, who had a shoeshine's bench at the foot of the Fonte Nova fountain, tended to act all high and mighty because he worked as a clerk in the town hall. All in all he amounted to one of those two-bit toffs who still earn less than us and blow it all on going about with a cloak and cane, mixing with learned gentlemen so they can all be Republicans, as they're called, and who meet sometimes in the park to give speeches that no one understands, until the Civil Guard moves them on. I was surprised to see him in Nonó's house, as I supposed he was at least a punter at Charity's or Monfortina's houses, which are, as you, Sir, have pointed out, and as I've already said, five-peseta houses.

'He murmured a grumpy "Good evening", as if it bothered him that we had seen him, and left through the back door, the way we had come in, which is the door trusted people use to come and go from the brothel. As he was leaving, he looked out of the corner of his eye at Gobs, who didn't even notice, what with the state he was in.

'Skinny went to see him out, and came back over beside me, and even gave me a kiss on the cheek, and huddled up next to me as if she were cold.

'I'd been busy with her a few times, as even though she wasn't particularly pretty or curvy, she was well known for her cleanliness and doing things well, which was true by the way... She had often suggested that we become lovers so that I wouldn't have to pay, 'cause as you, Sir, have pointed out, it's the custom here for the boyfriends to sleep over on Mondays without paying anything, although that's a swindle, 'cause whoever doesn't pay for the nooky is going to pay his bit for the dinner and drink and tip the blind man from Cudeiro too.

'"Ah, my prince!" Skinny said, giving me nips on the thighs, "you're certainly man enough to put a bun in ten women's ovens…! Come over here, you sponger! Shall we get dirty?"

'"Leave off, woman, I'm not in the mood. I'm very tired… And besides, you know that I can't stand being with a woman who has just been with another man."

'"Who? Him? Dear me! A load of sweet nothings and this, that and whatever, a pinch here and a pinch there, pawing all over your body, and he even does things that make you sick to think of them afterwards, and at the end of the day… bugger all, you're worse off than before… Shall we go? Look, Cibrán, after someone like him, I'm telling you that what I need is a man of your measurements, who gets down to business without messing around, and who even comes back for more… Shall we go?"

'"I've got no money!" I told her, to keep her quiet.

'"And so what? Pay me another day, I know your word is good."

'"No woman, no…"

'"Come on, man!" And lowering her voice, she added, almost speaking right into my ear: "When we're finished, go out alone by the front door without saying anything. It's no good for you to be seen with them… Come on and I'll tell you everything, as we might not have time later…"

'"Leave the man be," said Nonó at that point, getting up, and with that big man's voice she pulled out of the bottom of her chest and which had such an effect when you heard it, 'cause she hardly ever spoke out loud. "It's best that you clear off, I don't want any trouble. Now that the Corporal has seen you it's best that you skedaddle." She was looking at Gobs as she finished speaking. "Didn't he say anything to you?" she asked Skinny.

'"And what's he going to say?" she answered, trying to pretend, though you could easily see that some words stayed in her trap.

'"Right, get going, and that's that. That bloke's going to report you... He's angry with me 'cause he knows I want to turf him out of here for teaching the girls bad habits..."

'"But report us for what?" blurted out Menaplenty, exasperated.

'"Hah, cut the crap and enough talking: you know why better than I do. Get going, and that's that."

'Gobs broke away with a shove from Vigo Lola, and as he leaped to his feet he kicked the bowl of wine over which splashed onto the fire, making it hiss. Nonó shuffled out, her whole body moving like a mountain, and disappeared through a door.

'"What are you up to, you nasty fucking drunkard?" screeched Skinny, talking to Xanciño. '"This is what happens to us for letting criminals in. And she's to blame, going about with him like a bitch on heat..."

'Menaplenty leapt up and grabbed Skinny by the hair while Gobs gave her a wallop smack bang in the face, which made her keel over like a sack of spuds. When Vigo Lola went for her too with a chair held over her head, Nonó came back with her face all red, almost black with rage, and with an enormous bar in her hand, swinging it around fearlessly and letting it fall on everyone.

'"Get out of here, you bastards!" she shouted in a voice which was like thunder from heaven. The blows she dealt out were so hard that one of them just missed Bocas and smashed the table... It was then that the sitting room door opened and the men and women who were in the shindig appeared with the intention of jumping us. We threw ourselves out through the back door, all three of us piling on top of each other, as if we'd been spat out of there... Behind us, the yells of the giantess could be heard filling the whole of Santísima Trinidade Square:

'"Thieves, criminals, tramps…! Everybody grab those bastards…!"

'It had stopped raining and a cold north wind blew, taking my breath away. There wasn't a living soul in the streets. The moon was large and clear between the patchy light clouds. When we stopped running around Correxidor Square, the midnight bells could be heard in the watchtower of the Cathedral. We headed uphill with the intention of staying at Menaplenty's house, in Crebacús Street. Our legs weren't holding us up well 'cause of those sweet drinks that are so treacherous, as you well know, Sir.

'"Well that's us fucked!" said Gobs, stopping in the doorway. "Go where you want, but I'm not going into any house. Just in case…"

'"I'm not leaving you," replied Menaplenty, taking the other fella by the arm with that touch of bravery that moved me. With that mixture so typical of him, when he realises something only to skip over it in one of his mad turns, Gobs made a suggestion:

'"We've got to finish off the money that's left. It's a bad omen to go out on a bender and come back home even if it's only with a scrap of money. So let's carry on!"

'"Look… I'd go with you," I told them, "but the cold has brought the pain in my feet back and I can't stand it anymore. Everywhere's shut and I can't walk like that from one place to another… So, if you'll forgive me, I'm going to my mother's house as it's so near…"

'"It's up to you." said Gobs, '"but I'm telling you that if they get their hands on you… I'm sure that by now everything's spread through town one way or another… If you want we'll go to Ruddy's inn, as everyone who goes there is messed up in one way or another. Besides that, they're almost all from out of town, as you know. Today there's got to be a big crowd, as it's the day before the market of the seventh and a knees up with muleskinners and cattle traders often gets going there and lasts all night... If we win we'll go on the five o' clock train to Monforte for a few days until this racket has blown over, 'cause I've been in far worse ones than this and all in all it's always a lot of fuss over nothing... What's it to be?"

'I thought for a bit. Gobs was definitely right. I was in the same hole as they were, at least until I could talk about how things happened like I'm doing now, as you can see that I wasn't guilty of anything. Besides, I knew that as soon as I was alone the "feeling" was going to come over me all of a sudden and I couldn't manage alone 'cause I already had a lot of things on my mind.

'"Right, what's it to be? You don't have to bottle out, man... When you're among friends you have to let things follow their course right to the end," said Aladio, putting his hand on my shoulder.

'"Do what you want! What I want is to be in the warm and to take off my clogs. So let's get going."

'That's what I said, but it wasn't all true. The truth is that I was beginning to feel uneasy inside and wanted to go where there were people and noise being made, and to drink and drink before it took over, even if my ribs began to burn.

'"It's not a good idea to go until the inn has filled up with people who turn up in the evening. That'll be about an hour from now. Hold on a bit and we'll go somewhere to kill the time or to see if we can climb into some comfy nook or cranny."

'The way Gobs had of putting so much certainty into everything he said spurred me on and we began to walk down Fornos Street. The sky was clear and the cold got into the marrow of your bones, and you could see that it was going to freeze over. At the end of the street we found the parish fritter shop open, and Menaplenty, urging us forward a few steps, threw the blanket over his head and went in.

He came back shortly afterwards with a couple of bottles of country augardente. From a doorway, where we had retreated to let a few people by who were crossing Estrela Street, we saw that some of them were coming out of the fritter shop door and were gesturing towards where they supposed Menaplenty would have gone. Things were not going well... When they went back in, we quickened our step and got onto Tecelán Street which was very dark, as if the lights hadn't been lit. There we gave the first bottle such a long kiss that we emptied it. We needed it alright, 'cause I was ready to drop, what with one thing and another! 'Cause when this dismay comes over me I'm no good for anything, and I just want to hide away where nobody can see or hear me, and gnash my teeth and bite my knuckles until they bleed, 'cause not even that hurts me...'

'...'

'Yes, Sir, it's true, don't believe me if you don't want to... But when I start to talk about this misfortune that afflicts me and nobody else...

'So, the drink lifted me out of that, as always, as if I'd been tied up at first and then untied... Just like that. But this time it made me laugh too, without me knowing why. The other two, without knowing why I was laughing, began to laugh as well, and in no time at all the three of us were laughing so loudly that we couldn't stand upright and walked along together, linking arms, and instead of going forward we lurched ahead, laughing all the while, as if we was about to crash on the ground without even falling, which was something to truly admire.

'That bit of fun made us so happy inside that we didn't even realise what we were doing until they threw water on top of us from a house. Then we caught onto the fact that we were causing more racket than was good for us, and as we couldn't stop laughing we began to cover each other's mouths, which made us even more eager to get going, and we no longer knew what to do to handle it... Suddenly Gobs, who never forgot to keep an eye out around him as he was more used to these madcap escapades than we was, said that we had to quicken our step, but without running, 'cause it seemed that somebody had been spying on us and slipping into the pockets of darkness between the walls of the street. Perhaps it was the people from the fritter shop. He also talked of waiting for them and of fighting with them, but I put that right out of his head, as it was not the time to be getting into new scrapes.

'And without knowing how, we found ourselves in Instituto Street. In the middle of it, in the distance, you could see a policeman coming towards us at a gentle pace. The street was lit up by the moon and we couldn't cross it without being seen. So we gradually made our way onwards, in single file and clinging to the shadowy patches, and when we were in front of Santa Eufemia churchyard, we saw that the church was open and we scurried in there like mice...

'The high altar shone, lit up by candles, and I was struck as to how this could be at such a late hour of the night. Surrounding it were two or three dozen gentlemen (there were no women to be seen), all of them kneeling, and the murmur of prayers said in low voices could be heard, and all of them close together and praying out loud, as if they was saying a litany, like those of the missions or rogations... There was no way I could tiptoe along in those damned iron-shod clogs without them making a noise on the flagstones. One of those gentlemen must have noticed something because he turned to take a look, but we were already hidden behind one of the columns, next to a confession booth.

'At that moment, the door squeaked a little and we saw the policeman, who was that bloke Sardine by the way, stick his nose out a bit, but he didn't budge from there. Though he couldn't see us where we were, we got into the confession box just in case and at the same moment when that damned laughter threatened to come over us again. That Sardine bloke stared for a moment and then went off, slowly pulling the door shut. We stayed there for a bit, waiting to see if he would go away or come back to stick his nose in again, and meanwhile we started on the second carafe of augardente, which was as strong as the first and seemed to have some charm of its own that made us so damned merry.

'"Those are the ones they say belong to the Nocturnal Worship, and pray only at night," said Menaplenty, who knew everything.

'After a little while, we popped our heads out to see if it was time for us to leave. And it was then that the damned laughter came back, but this time for a good reason, as we saw that all those gentlemen were no longer kneeling but almost bending forward, with their buttocks raised and their heads lowered, almost touching the ground, all of them belting out a song as if they were growling it through their noses.

'Menaplenty was the first to start letting out that shameless hussy's giggle of his, which suddenly rose to a cackle, as he'd been holding it in for a good while. And as if his laughter was all that was needed to set us off, fuck it, an explosion of chuckles came after that gave me a stitch in the side that wouldn't let me breathe, and what with a bit of laughing and another bit of drinking, we almost didn't make it over to where the door was. And if that wasn't enough, When Gobs, that liability who among other bad habits had the reputation of being a farter, reached the door, he let rip one of those long ones, begging your pardon, which end with a thunderclap.'

'...'

'Let me laugh, Sir, as something funny had to come to mind among so many ugly and sad things from that outlandish night.'

' ...'

'And what other events, Sir? Those are the events, and it happened just like that. They ended because other things had been going on before. If they hadn't happened, the end would be a different way to what it was. 'Cause the truth is that what we did wasn't the kind of thing you normally get up to on a bender, 'cause at the end of the day it was all just a bit of fun and pranks which can be sorted out... We kept doing it without even realising, at least as far as I'm concerned, except that afterwards there was no way of putting it right, like someone who keeps locking doors behind himself and throwing away the keys, as if he didn't want to come back, just like we were walking towards our doom.'

' ...'

'As regards the "procedures", well as you, Sir, have pointed out, after walking for a while on leaving the church, we stopped for a bit to get that laughter out which was choking us, and then we reached the Rei fountain where we pissed in the basin, begging your pardon. And it was then, and I'm telling you 'cause of the importance the matter had later on, that Gobs began to talk to what he had in his hand, begging your pardon, Sir, telling it very affectionately that "it wasn't going to go home empty handed", that "benders don't end without a woman", for it "to be patient", and other nonsense like that, which even made me feel ashamed to hear it from the mouth of fully-grown man, though you have to understand that the booze does these things.

'So it was there that Gobs started stirring up that obsession again, that we had to go to see the lord of Andrada's beautiful mysterious lady once more... And neither I nor Menaplenty could get such a mad idea out of his skull, 'cause we already knew that Gobs was like that, as temperamental as a little kid, and when something got into his head he had to do it, even if his life were at stake, 'cause I for one never knew a man as fearless as him.'

'...'

'It's fine, yes, Sir. It'll be just as you prefer, as long as you leave me here and don't take me to the cells. No, not that...!'

'...'

'I don't need... Even if I had to die of hunger. Apart from that, I've no damned appetite for food... Though a nip of red wine, to warm me up a little...

'Thank you very much, Sir! Thank you very much!'

CHAPTER FOUR

'...'

'No, Sir, no. When the scuffle flared up in Ruddy's inn, we'd already left. We hung around close by without letting anybody see us, to keep an eye on what was happening.'

'...'

'Yes, Sir, we saw that they were taking out the wounded guy from Zamora, and you could see his bleeding face. Then others came out, all embroiled in a huge scrap with sticks and huge knives.'

'...'

'No, Sir, no. I'll tell you again... We've already got enough on our plate without having to be burdened with things that we didn't do... We lost our money in a game of blackjack that some ham traders from Maside had got going, and they're people quite taken to sponging and getting up to no good around the fairs, with loaded decks. I told Gobs but he didn't pay any attention...'

'...'

'How do you expect me to know the names? I'm saying this because some fellas from Ribeiriño who I met there told me.'

'...'

'No, Sir, I don't know what they're called either... I know they're from Ribeiriño 'cause I've seen them there, in Sacristan's inn.'

'...'

'Well we went back towards town. We went up the Trives road and got onto the Travesía without seeing anyone... Gobs kept going on about his fixation, and was now even more set on it because we'd no money left.'

'...'

'I don't think so, though I couldn't swear to it. Who knows what goes on inside every one of us! The obsession from the start seemed to be to see the beautiful lady once again. Maybe after the first time...'

'...'

'Sir, I'm begging you not to make me say what I didn't say... I said that he'd no money left and nothing more, and that perhaps 'cause of that he went back to the idea of us going to the Andrada house again... Maybe if we'd left the gambling den with plenty of money, he would've got the urge to do other things, I reckon... but I wasn't inside his head to know that...

'So when we got near the town square, we heard the Cathedral clock strike three. The frost was spread over the streets and the rooftops, and everything was like glass 'cause of the bright moonlight, and the puddles of rain were once again hardened by ice. When we went through the park you could still see the glow of the fire at the manor and it troubled me a lot to see it, as I'd already forgotten about it... Or at least I hadn't thought about it. Then I was filled with great anxiety and got the urge to leave my friends and go do I don't know what. But Gobs didn't give me any time to think. When he got something in his... He went in front of us, walking confidently on, without saying a word, and we followed him, reluctantly on my part, but we followed him as if instead of going in front he was behind, pushing us along.

'I had no doubt that the new folly we were going to put into action would put the "feeling" once again into my body, 'cause I could already feel it coming up through my chest from below, sapping my energy and getting right into my thoughts, only to scatter them about, as always. I'm telling you, Sir, that this stupefaction of my thoughts, this darkness that slowly fills up my brain like a smoke cloud, I don't know how to explain it... 'Cause at least when I was a boy, when these things happened to me, though I'd still not managed to call them the "feeling" yet, at least they got shorter with the fainting, which was just like going to sleep... And even when I was regaining my senses, even if I was all bruised and sometimes injured, they would even squeeze my fingers with instruments and pull my tongue out so I couldn't swallow it, and once it was over I'd feel very well with that lightness in my body as if I was waking up from a very long dream, and even for a bit after that I didn't remember what had happened... But now...

'Well, either way we were in that mess and we had to keep going. I certainly wished I could be free of the whole business, 'cause when things outside me are very strong they can overcome those inside, and I begin to get over the "feeling", which tries to get me on my own in order to come at me more furiously, well I have to act like it's not there and go around with people or do things to escape it, so that I'm stronger on the outside, as if all that were going to drive me mad...'

'...'

'You're more than right, Sir... But the thing is, when I start to talk about this desperate business which happens to me, I can never stop. And perhaps all this talking is to see if I can understand myself, as I often talk away without talking to anyone in particular, as if I were two people instead of one.

'Well, getting back to the matter in hand, I had to go slowly because of my chilblains, which what with the cold weather were hurting like hell. The other two went on ahead arguing all the while. They weren't really involved in a shouting match as such, but Aladio Menaplenty was babbling on and on as if he were talking to a wall, while we strode on without answering him, his hands stuffed in his pockets, throwing a "For the love of God!" at him every now and again and at the same time looking like he wanted to belt him, as this was the way they always carried on... And that's how we got into Burga Alley. When we reached the hollow of the earthworks, Menaplenty still wanted to stop him by grabbing him by the wrist, but Gobs, without saying anything, gave him a knock on his wounded neck and he fell, smacking his chops on the ground.

'Without a doubt, Gobs was more out of it than I had ever seen him before. He was so wrapped up in his obsession that, rather than drunk, 'cause he'd drunk twice as much as the two of us put together, he seemed mad, a writhing and cantankerous madman who was as frightening as a lunatic. The drink didn't soften Xanciño, no matter how much he'd put away, and instead, as he kept drinking he'd become sterner, harder, moodier, till when he couldn't stand any more he'd suddenly fall asleep as if he were dead. And then he would sleep for days at a time and nobody could wake him up. But until the time came for him to calm down in this way, he proved to be very much in control of himself, even if he seemed fearless and provocative, as if he wanted to fight with everyone who looked at him. But all this and speaking and moving about normally, as if he wasn't drunk, which was something you could only tell by the ruddiness of his face, which would turn as white as linen, and that glow in his eyes, but above all in his acting all stern and fearless just like a wild beast, doing whatever he liked without seeing sense and knocking down everything that stood in his path. His drunkenness could be seen more in the things that he'd do than how he'd do them, which was a serious undertaking with all kinds of shenanigans and madness, perhaps too serious, although though for those of us who knew him when he was sober he was losing control of himself with those urges that got into him.

'So he got into the hole by the earthworks and began to straighten the rungs which had acted as a ladder for us to climb into the Andrada garden that morning. He felt his way along, guiding himself by the slight glow that came in through the upper part of the hole. I made some suggestions to him that we shouldn't get ourselves into that mess again; just 'cause it had turned out alright for us once didn't mean it wouldn't go pear-shaped now, 'cause that's the way things are. Gobs, without stopping, replied:

'"I'm not telling you both to come if you're frightened. In fact, I'm telling you that it's best that you don't come. I want to be with this woman even if I have to risk my life or take the life from whoever gets in my way, even if I have to knock down half the world. And that's that... So now you know..."

'"Shut it, you fool, shut it," murmured Menaplenty. "You'd think that she'd already agreed to marry you... What you'll get from all this is them ridding you of the handful of brain cells you've got left with a few blasts from a shotgun. Come on, you. He can go fuck himself with his obsessions."

'"In this situation," I answered him, "I won't leave a friend no matter how much I can't stand what he's doing, like now with this big horse who isn't capable of anything else but coming up with harebrained escapades. Either we're all out of here or we're all climbing up, come what may, 'cause as far as I'm concerned I don't want anybody to have the right to call me a bottler afterwards..."

'But by now Gobs had begun to crawl up the side of the hole, driving in the rungs as he went. We had no other choice but to follow him. So that's what we did...

'The house was completely in darkness, as was to be expected. The grove of camellias cast a thick and fearful shadow that was carved on the ground. The moon was slowly waning, and its glow made all the windows of the gallery sparkle like mirrors… I'm telling you, Sir, that such silence and fearful brightness made me more afraid than a dozen armed men would have done. It seemed as if something were bound to happen any second…

'Pressing ourselves against the wall, we gradually reached the lower part of the house. Gobs began to weigh up where we thought he could get upstairs, pushing the doors and fiddling with latches without any kind of care. One of them gave, and we went in, lighting matches, and we saw the garage, which was all full of dust and cobwebs that hung everywhere and which got in our faces as we walked. From there we entered a kind of wine cellar or pantry stuffed full of things to eat and drink. Xanciño, acting as if he weren't in somebody else's house, lit up an oil lamp, rolled a fag, looking as cool as a cucumber all around and noticed a bottle which was there on a table, half empty, tidily placed upon a tray and with a small glass next to it. Each of us took a good swig and it turned out to be a sweet and sticky liqueur, tasting of sugared anisette, but with a taste like a chemist's concoction, though it was easily drinkable, and in the end it warmed the body as well as the finest augardente. On the shelves of the walls there were many tins of food with writing that you couldn't understand and a great many bottles with foreign names too, as far as we could see. On the same tray there was a lump of little rosary beads, like shotgun pellets and which, by the looks of it, must have been some kind of food. I grabbed a pinchful and then spat them out, as they tasted of rotten fish.

'After being there a while we sat down, as relaxed as if we were guests. Gobs and Menaplenty even cut some good slices from a ham that had been started on, and opened a few bottles without blinking an eye. I wasn't hungry at first and continued to that syrup that tasted of medicine, so that it soothed my throat and warmed my cockles, bless my soul. Then I gnawed on a bit of summer sausage and drank from one of those bottles, which turned out to be a mature wine, lighter and sharper than what we were used to drinking.

'Gobs went a little further into the house, carrying the oil lamp and holding up his hand so that the light didn't shine in his face. He did that so sure of himself that I realised it was not the first time that he'd done such things. He came back straight away, and from the door he gestured for us to follow him. We began to walk through a long corridor and came across a large doorway, made of wood, and from where a stairway emerged, very wide and long, and everything was covered with one of those thick cloths which absorbed the sound of the steps as if you were walking over a muddy field. On reaching the landing above, we were given one hell of a fright, as there were two of those iron men that are in school books, who are called knights-in-armour, and even though you know that they're hollow inside, they make anyone who's never seen them up close afraid at first.

'On the walls there were a load of those weapons from times when the Moors were abroad, which can be seen through the windows of many a fancy house, 'cause I've seen them too, and they're often very clean and tidily set out, and you could see that they were there to make the place look more fancy, as they often do in posh houses, where they hang everything up on the wall.

'Gobs went up to a chest that was there and which we thought would have nothing inside it, but we opened it, and he took for himself the longest and most dazzling sword, and gave each one of us one of those thingamajigs, though I don't know what use it had, 'cause as far as I was concerned, I was busy keeping an eye on where we were walking, so that I could start run back as soon as anybody appeared, as I'm the kind who doesn't want any trouble, and though the drink had gone to my head, it wasn't enough not to make me realise that what we were about to do was more like being bandits than young men who had grown up in the town and who are out on a bender.

'So, with one thing and another, and after we'd walked through those long corridors without hearing a living soul, a band of light emerged from beneath a door. Gobs, not paying much attention to the sabre that he carried in his hand, took out his knife, just in case, and pushed the door open without any kind of care. The light came from a lamp or candlestick holding church candles, three of which were lit but now almost going out, while one was unlit. Everything that was in that bedroom, 'cause that's what it was as could be seen by the bed, seemed like something from a church, with great cloths hanging from paintings of saints and even carved wooden saints, and sculptures, and hung above the bedstead there was even a large statue of Christ, just like a real man, who even appeared to be looking at us through a crack in his eyelids. Some half-burnt heather branches were smouldering in the chimney and you could smell a soft and pleasant aroma in the air that seemed more like medicine than perfume.

'In the middle of the bedroom you could see an armchair whose back was facing where we had come in. And it was there that we were given a second fright, as we saw that from one side hung a man's arm. We came to an abrupt halt and Gobs cleared his throat and spat to see if he would move. But he didn't move one bit. Then he moved towards him slowly, until he was right next to the chair and shaking his head right next to what he saw.

'When we went over we saw that there, completely laid out like a dead man, was the bearded gentleman we'd seen that morning. He was lying against a large pillow and covered from head to toe in what looked like a bishop's habit. Dribble dripped from a corner of his mouth, and his eyes were glazed over and still, so that he might well have been inebriated as much as deceased... Gobs, without any shred of fear, poked the tip of the thingamajig in his beard without the other fella showing the slightest sign of life, and turning his face towards us, Gobs murmured:

'"He's as pissed as a fart."

'But no drink of any description could be seen there, though he could also have drunk somewhere else and gone there to sleep it off.

'On the small table beside him there was a bed warmer as small as a plate and also a pipe or something like that, as small as a seamstress' thimble, but I don't know what the hell you could've smoked in that. The pipe had a stinking mixture stuck at the bottom, like tar, and I realised that it gave off the same smell that was floating in the air, though it was stronger and smellier... We also realised that the bed there was not a double one...

'While Gobs and I were caught up in these things, Menaplenty had started to fiddle about with a piece of furniture that looked like a chest stood up on its side, all full of intricate little drawers, like a toy. When I saw that he was taking some jewellery out of them, I went over to stop him from doing such a thing, 'cause as I've said before it's one thing being out on a booze-up and another to be a swindler. But Gobs got in between us and the two of them began to poke around in the little drawers, which was when they came across the ounces of gold that they found in Gobs' pockets... 'Cause Gobs gave all the jewellery to the other fella, except some earrings and a gorgeous ring which he no doubt thought to give to Vigo Lola... I'm not trying to act all innocent now, but you must believe me that I wasn't involved in all this thieving shenanigans, 'cause nothing was found on me that wasn't mine anyway, as you well know, Sir, and as I already said at the police station, even though those criminals laid into me to their heart's content so that I'd tell them where I'd hidden the things... Yes, Sir, it was them and nobody else, and they even started off on the job in complete agreement, only to start a scrap over the loot when more of it began to appear [I don't follow], so that you couldn't bear to listen to them... As soon as I saw them like that, so brazen and determined when they were stealing, I realised that they weren't the boys I thought I knew well (even with their weaknesses that so typical of young lads who like to go on a bender), but people who were used to these kinds of schemes and dealings...

'So, taking advantage of them being as busy as gypsies dividing up the booty, I began to creep away, and when I realised that I was by the door I took off my clogs with one jerk, which was like my soul being ripped from my body, and, grabbing one of the stubs from the candlestick, I left determined to escape whichever way I could... I got a little lost in one of those corridors, which gave them time to catch me. And when they caught me they had a go at me for wanting to clear off without them, and they even claimed that I'd grabbed something for myself, something really valuable, and when I heard that I had the urge to jump on them and kick their teeth in so they wouldn't think we were all like them and so that they didn't act like bastards, begging your pardon. When they'd searched me and convinced themselves that I wasn't carrying anything, I told them:

'"I'm free to go, and you can do what the hell you like... It's up to you! For a start, I want to clear off because I'm not a thief, and secondly 'cause that man, or other people that might be in the house, might wake up, and you, Xanciño, are man enough to get up to any mischief of the kind that can't be sorted out, I know you only too well, though I didn't know you well enough to think that you were this sly... So let me go, 'cause you both know that I've got a temper too." We were saying all this in a low voice in a corner of a corridor.

'"Wait a second, man," murmured Gobs, speaking in a different tone, almost politely, but going back to his godforsaken obsession. "You know very well that I came here to be with that woman. What I took doesn't matter to me, and I'll give them to you if you want, so that you'll realise... But I'm not leaving without being with that woman. When we find her it won't bother me whether you lot clear off. But for now I'm begging you not to go, OK?"

'He babbled it all out just like a madman, and I'm telling you, Sir, that though I'm not the kind of man who gets frightened by anything, it was frightening to hear that man in the light thrown out by the candle stub, with that determination in his demented eyes, as if he were able in that moment to charge alone against a dozen men if they stood in his way. Menaplenty, either 'cause he was afraid too, or because of that fury that came over him when the other fella would talk about women, began to growl:

'"He's right, that fella, he's right... Let's get going now, don't be stubborn. With what we've got there's enough to sort everything out... Let's get going, for Christ's sake..."

'But Xanciño wasn't seeing straight. Already, in the course of the day, you could tell that each time he got the subject into his head, his face began to look as if he really had been struck with madness. He would grind his teeth until his jaw shook and struggled for air as if he couldn't breathe. And his eyes would cloud over, opaque and tiny, just like when he drew his knife in scrapes and rumbles in pubs... In the end, the only thing you got from contradicting him was that the mad irritation that had made him restless all day, from the very moment when we'd seen the lady, would come over him even stronger, and I curse the moment when that finally happened.

'So, without paying us the slightest attention, he began to go back down the corridor, swearing and making threats at the top of his voice, kicking at the doors which opened without any effort, and you could see that none of them had any latches. We went into two of those rooms and there wasn't a soul to be seen. By the looks of it there was nobody In that house... and as far as I'm concerned I would have preferred somebody to appear, no matter who they were, and to go at it with fist and knife against everyone instead of that silence, and so many floors full of valuable things, of tables set as if for big meals and beds made, wide and luxurious, in which nobody slept, and everything lit up...

'Gobs, with his teeth clenched and his breath whistling, lifted up the bedclothes with his sword, and jabbed at the curtains hanging over doorways, opened cupboards with a single wrench... And on it went like that from one moment to the next until we went into the gallery we'd seen that morning from outside.

'Inside it was very spacious and stuffed with plants, and the branches of one of them crept upwards until they covered the ceiling. The full moon was shining brightly on the windows. We doused the light we had with us and everything was plunged into that twilight which was pale like something from a ghost story.

'"Let's go, Xan, let's go now that we're here," I begged him in a firm voice. "As it stands, this can't turn out well. The gallery is lower down and we can easily jump..."

'It was then that we saw approaching from within the house and from the bottom of the corridor, lights that moved. Gobs closed the door, taking the key out of the lock, and we began to walk quickly in search of the end of the gallery where we supposed it would be easier to go down. By now an uproar of voices could be heard behind the door and somebody shaking it to jolt it open. And it was at that very moment that Xan, who was in front, stopped all of a sudden and then pulled back towards us, stammering:

'"There she is, there she is…"

'Indeed, behind some thick and large clumps of leaves, the beautiful lady could be seen bathed in moonlight, sitting facing the garden, just as we had seen her that morning, with her arms outstretched, and her eyes still and shining, like the most beautiful thing we had ever seen in this world. We stopped so close to her that we were afraid even to breathe. My heart beat so hard in the box of my chest that I was sure that it could be heard… She was sat in a wheelchair and had a small boy in her lap. Gobs took a step forward, coming out from behind the leaves, and went over beside her, saying:

'"Madame, don't be afraid, as we mean you no harm…" We were expecting her to let out a cry as soon as she saw us, but she didn't move or utter a word in response. Menaplenty, who was stuck to me, was shaking like a reed in the wind and I was sweating as if it were the depths of summer. We were so shocked that by now the knocks on the door and the sound of an old woman's voice shouting no longer bothered us, and we didn't know what she was saying:

'"*Voler, voler; secur, secur*…!" or something like that.

'Xanciño was staring at the lady, completely still, amazed and with a smile that looked like a child's pout when they're about to start crying, but the lady didn't blink nor did she move; it was as if she was dead.

'"Madame…!" he even said to her, daring to take one of her hands. But he didn't do it very well, and threw it off with a jolt as if he'd gone and burnt himself. With this movement the child fell to the floor and smashed into pieces against the tiles. Gobs, by now recovered, struck her, grabbing her roughly by the nape of her neck as if he were about to hit her, and the lady went completely to one side without bending, her arms always stiff and her hands open.

'"Fuck me! What a mad fucker I am!" shouted Gobs. And with a tremendous kick to the chair, he threw the lady to the floor, and there she lay in the same way as when she was sitting, her lifeless eyes shining with the moonlight. After taking two steps away he came back again, raging mad, and sank his heel two or three times into the doll's face leaving a hole, dark and fearsome, like a smashed skull.

'And with that, we reached the end of the gallery where we found a stairway that led to the orchard, and went down it almost in one leap. We crossed the garden when we saw people with lights who were coming into the gallery. We got down any way we could through the tunnel and began to creep off without pausing for breath until we were near the station…'

'...'

'No, Sir, we went to the Campo das Bestas after that. First off, we went in the direction of the station. I don't know if I already said that we'd thought of catching the passenger and goods train which passes, as you, Sir, point out, at five in the morning, and for us to go to Monforte until the matter had blown over a bit, as time sorts everything out. And if it didn't, we also talked about going on to that part of Asturias where apparently good work could be found in the coal mines, and Gobs had some good friends there.

'But when we crossed the Roman Bridge I came across Fatso, the fella who owned a ragman's cart, which he was hitching up in front of his house. Fatso thinks a lot of me 'cause he was a friend of my father when they worked as sweepers in Cadiz. He came out from behind the mules, when the others had already gone past, as I'd gradually fallen behind 'cause of my feet, and he took me aside to tell me that we'd best not be going to the station as a pair of Civil Guard were knocking around there looking for us. He also told me that we should clear off as soon as possible, as what we'd done had already spread around town... although naturally he didn't know everything, of course. But he told me that as well as the matter of Gobs with Balbino Onions in Chaguazoso's pub, they were putting the fire in the manor down to us, which they say was amazing, as they couldn't recall there having been such a big one for many years. They thought the distiller was dead 'cause he was so scorched, and it had burnt a load of livestock and pigs that had been in the sties ready for slaughter, as well as other damage that the fire did in the manor itself, and that if they caught us they were going to beat us to death without waiting for the law, and whatever and whatnot...

'So I thanked him once I'd told him that the business wasn't as bad as people were wittering on about, and I went over to the others to tell them. Gobs wanted to play down the matter straightaway, but in spite of that we turned on our heel. Going over the top of the Roman Bridge again, a jolt of "feeling" came into my head so suddenly and savagely that I wasn't far off jumping from the wall to throw myself into the river. I almost did it, 'cause for a brief moment I was no longer in control of myself... I think that the cold that hit my temples and that weakness in my legs saved me, as if I were about to pass out... It's a good job it went away...

'When we reached the other side of the bridge, Menaplenty got two fine bottles of augardente (which we really needed if we were not going to pass out) from Sacristan's pub, which is quite nearby and which was preparing for the market on the seventh, and soon the traders would start to arrive. We saw one of them off straightaway like water from the fountain, without even stopping, 'cause there are times like that when you drink not 'cause of the drink but as if you're getting some medicine down you, so that you wouldn't collapse through lack of strength...

'At that moment I no longer knew what to do with myself and felt lost. I thought about my mother, the kid, Raxada, as if I were remembering them from beyond the grave. I'd changed in so many ways in such a short space of time that I was now no longer the same person, the man that I'd wanted to be the day before, when I decided to make up with my girl and to live a good life as a hard-working man, supporting myself and my family. Misfortune had turned up on the road in the company of those good-for-nothings and I was forced to get involved in things I'd never done or thought of doing. And the greatest pity was that this was going to happen to me just when I'd decided to become a decent man, as if bad fortune had come to stop me in my attempt just as I was getting going. But now it's all fucked up, 'cause of me and my bad luck...!'

'...'

'Yes, Sir, yes. I realise that it's no use moaning about it now, but it helps me a little, getting rid of this weight in my heart that seems to want to drown me, and this coming and going of the "feeling", which has hardly left me since they brought me here... And what without any drink to help me recover from this suffocation... And just as well that you, Sir, have been so good and didn't let them take me back to the police station, 'cause then the "feeling" would have ended up driving me mad... You have to realise that a young fella, who is every inch a man, can't stand another man who isn't his father laying a hand on his face without him taking offence and without being able to return the favour, all handcuffed like they've got me, and I've no idea how there can be Christian men so horrible and degenerate that they hit other men who've done nothing to them and who can't fight back, 'cause that's not justice nor anything damned well like it what was done to me, begging your pardon, and what I've said means no disrespect to you, Sir...'

'...'

'You're right Sir... Excuse me... But you don't know what it's like to find yourself in the hands of some bastard layabout who, just 'cause he's wearing a uniform, goes along and bashes a man who everybody knows and who's a local, landing wallops in your face or whipping your back, and even kicks you where the sun don't shine, not to mention the bollocks, begging your pardon, like you were a gypsy. And on top of that laughing and taking the mickey out of you, which is the same as them hitting you right in the depths of your soul, which is where it hurts most, and most of all 'cause they have you chained like an animal without you being able to move... And I swear, Sir, that if I have to go to prison, I'll go, and if I have to do hard labour, I'll do it, 'cause whoever did wrong has to pay for it even though he did it without meaning to... But if you send me back to the police station, I swear on my mother's life...'

'...'

'You're more than right, Sir, and God bless you for your patience with me, you're quite considerate for somebody who's not from here, and not like that son of a bitch sergeant, who I'm not surprised is from the Maragatería...'

'...'

'No, Sir, the cat hasn't got my tongue... The thing is that your way of shouting at me has gone and pissed me off, 'cause I've said nothing against you, nor did I think anything of the sort, as God is my witness... And if I let slip some swear word or the like, you have to consider the situation of a man who, no matter what has happened, has never been involved with the law, and so many hours without seeing anybody, except for those bastards, without eating, without drinking, with them knocking me around all over the place, asking me questions without letting me say a word, giving me a bloody big slap in the mouth when I want to say something, without even being able to ask for a drop of water, without being able to do my business without them being in front of me...'

'...'

'Yes, Sir, I understand now, and I'll do it straightaway, just as you say Sir...

'...well, those drops of augardente boosted our strength once again, though less than before, 'cause the things we had to drown out with the drink were getting even stronger. I'd already realised that I couldn't keep drinking 'cause my stomach was already rotten and the others seemed to be as wasted as I was... They went in front, as always, arms around each other's waist and wanting to pretend that they were happy and that it was all to do with the bender and would go away just as other commotions and escapades had on other occasions...

'We were walking along some out-of-the way tracks which we got onto through the middle of the vineyards on the outskirts of town, and Menaplenty's voice could be heard, with his stammering chit-chat like the sentimental muck spoken by young couples. They walked along with the unsteady pace of drunkards, with the blanket thrown over their heads and poking, tickling and pushing each about like it was perfectly normal. It was then that Menaplenty took advantage of the state that the other fella was in, 'cause when Xanciño was in control of his own faculties he wouldn't be doing with it, or at least he wouldn't let himself get up to that filthy business which isn't for real men, and as far as I can tell, having knocked about so much with them, I could never work out if he drank so the other fella could take advantage of him, or if Menaplenty made him drink to take advantage. But what I can say is that neither of them would get drunk without the other, and that they'd never been seen drunk when not in each other's company, or in anybody else's company, and that stuff was one big mystery that was talked about in pubs. But when they got sozzled, sooner or later they'd end up with that horrible tomfoolery of hugging and hitting each other, and not a soul could understand it.

'It was bastard cold. My feet hurt as if the skin had been peeled off them, and I was even scared of the prospect of taking off my shoes again and seeing the damage that I'd done with so much walking, with the chilblains gnawed by the clogs and my socks caked with the blood and pus of my wounds...

'So there came a moment when I couldn't go on and I let myself fall beside a wall, at God's mercy, as I no longer cared about anything... I felt a great weakness in my body and was all in a daze, and I didn't know if it was tiredness, pain or the drink. When the others realised, they came back for me and carried me along, almost dragging me by my arms, and Gobs said to buck me up that we were now close to shelter where he knew that we could lie low to rest up and talk about what had to be done, without us being out in the open for them to see us.

'Gobs was acting very strange. One minute he was happy and full of confidence, the next doubtful and morose. You couldn't trust him much, 'cause he was a very shrewd man and capable of greater deceit. Besides that, he was, out of the three of us, the one who was most out of his head, to the extent that he seemed completely drunk at times, both in the way he walked and talked... The obsession he'd had all day, and which became even stronger once night had fallen, was being with a woman, and we couldn't get him out of it. And since he'd missed out on the business with the lady who'd turned out to be a doll, that fixation had got stronger in his head... 'Cause when Gobs got stubborn he was like an animal, save for his blessed soul, and there was nobody who could stop him. His eyes, which were normally like a child's, would shrink and turn hard and glare just like those of a wild beast, and when he spoke at all it was through his teeth, with his jaws clamped tight like he was mumbling instead of talking, and you had to concentrate as hard as you could in order to catch what he was saying.

'Menaplenty was moaning too, 'cause the wound from the bite had been irritated even more by the cold and brought out a red blister on his neck, surrounded by trickles of congealed blood. With his drunkard's stuttering talk, Gobs was saying:

'"Soddit! I want to be with a woman who isn't a whore! If you were good friends to me…"

'"You don't half need it!" replied the other fella, his voice a mix of mockery and spite.

'And we carried on like that, stumbling along that track which seemed to have no end… They would stop every so often and take a slug from the bottle, and I don't know how those bodies could take so much. The Poofter, who seemed to be the most delicate, was the one who could take the most out of the three of us. Gobs, after each swig, would hawk loudly like he had fire in his throat, and let out his filthy whine again:

'"…I've already told you I want to be with a woman who isn't a whore…!"

'"How are you going to do that if you've no strength left, you lazy bastard? What do you want a woman for? Go on, give this one a kiss…" And he stuck the carafe against his teeth, and spilt more on his clothes than what he swallowed.

'I was walking in between them and after a while I began to get loose from them, although I preferred to follow them as best I could. A strong aroma of augardente and the perfume that Menaplenty had put on from a bottle that he'd robbed in the house of the mad gentleman followed them, and that mixture of smells made me sick to the pit of my stomach, 'cause everything seemed to reek of the same thing: the air, clothes, the smoke from the fag… Suddenly Xan stopped and stood gazing sideways for a while, and as if a new idea had come to him, he leapt over a hedge and, without saying anything, began to walk along a path that crossed the Abade das Vellas farm. 'Cause of the way he took to the road, with long strides, almost running, I realised that in fact another mad idea had got into his head. He'd often do that: as soon as a whim came over him he didn't even think about it and followed it through as soon as possible. And the riskier it was, the quicker he got down to it. That was what he was like now: steady, resolved, determined, and even his walk straightened out as if he hadn't been drinking, and it was hard work keeping up with him.

'That's how we reached Campo das Bestas, which is kind of, as you, Sir, point out, the place where the sweepers go to empty the rubbish from the city.

'The ground was sodden in part by the rain that had fallen, and more so by the piles of fresh rubbish, and our feet sank up to the ankles in that filthy mud that stank to high heaven. The lower parts were hard and slippery because of the ice, so it was best to walk on top of the rubbish.

'In the middle of Campo das Bestas the land forms a marsh or pond, quite deep and made by the rainwater, and which in summertime fills up with midges and horseflies and gives off a smell which stinks all round those parts, and they even say that a few plagues have started there. Now it was frozen between the piles of rubbish and it shone like a misted mirror 'cause of the moon, which had by now almost disappeared behind Santa Ladaíña hill but was still hanging on a bit.

'Though I didn't say anything, when we got to that place I began to suspect what that bad fella had planned, even though I couldn't believe it.

'In a hut that's down there, a little further back from the edge of the rubbish ground and half-covered by some young birch trees, lived Socorrito, the mad woman... I suppose that you've already met her, Sir, 'cause anyone who's been in our city for a bit ends up meeting her and liking her. She's still quite a young woman: tall, well-built and pretty, in spite of the damage done to the poor girl by the life she's led. She'd turned up a few years ago on the streets of Auria, just like those mad people who turn up from God knows where, with a child of rags held against her chest, pretending to breastfeed it. When she came here, Socorrito's skin was delicate and pale, her hair curly and dark, and instead of hanging down it was tied up in ringlets around her head like a crown. Her voice was very soft and she always spoke Castilian, as peasant women often do when they lose their minds. She looked like a lady from town, with her clothes so well fitted and with those gentle movements and that smile with perfect white teeth... Within no time at all everybody loved her lots and around the houses they would give her food and clothes, though it wouldn't be easy for her to admit it as she used to say that she wasn't one to go around the fairs begging, but that she was used to eating at a set table, with a white tablecloth and served by maids; but everything was a fantasy and it was the imagination of her madness that made her go like that... And as for her clothes, for every item they gave her they had to give her another one for her child, even though she would be quite happy with any old bit of cloth which wouldn't be enough even to cover a finger. And when she accepted things she never said thank you, though she was always very courteous, just like a well-to-do lady, and would say that her housekeeper would soon order 'the bill to be paid...' Poor old Socorrito! A few good people tried to grab her and take her to the asylum, but when that happened she tended to faint and even fall ill and her character would turn very irritable, so they had to let her go again... So she'd go back to that hut, where the council sweepers kept the carts and brooms, and where she lived surrounded by cradles that they'd given to her as charity, or which the carpenters would make for her with four planks, or that she'd put together with boxes that she took, 'cause they said she must've had twenty children, each one by a different man and all boys... It's said that she went mad when she lost her honour to a Portuguese sawyer who forced himself on her when she was still a girl in the place where she was from, which was around Lobeira or somewhere like that... The strapping lads of Auria would make harmless fun of her 'cause of her obsession with wanting to be a mother to so many sons, and we'd ask her, speaking in Castrapo too:

'"Socorrito, when are we going to make a baby together?" And she, without stopping smiling, would go over to who'd asked her the question, and after smelling him for a bit, would reply:

'"I can't have a son of yours because you smell bad. Do excuse me!"

'However, when a gentleman would walk past her, a good-looking and well-dressed lad, even if he were with his wife, she'd go up to him and say affectionately:

'"Don't you smell well! When are you going to give me a baby?"

'"Tomorrow, Socorrito, tomorrow, I'm in a hurry today," was the charitable and often tender reply they gave her. Some stranger, when it happened to him, even winced after what they'd told him of the matter. Poor old Socorrito!'

'...'

'I already realised that you must've known her, Sir, and that I wasn't telling you anything new, but in the middle of so much crap I was enjoying getting started on her story 'cause of...'

'...'

'That's fine, yes, Sir... So Gobs went and asked Menaplenty for the bottle of perfume, and sprayed himself with all what was left. Then he took another gulp from the bottle and tossed it, empty, far away from him. And with that he began to walk with his legs open wide, trying to steady himself.

'"Where are you going in that state?" shouted Menaplenty, 'cause by the looks of it he didn't have a clue. didn't reply and kept walking, tripping over piles of rubbish. "Wait, I'm coming with you…"

'"You're not coming anywhere," replied Xan, stopping for a moment, and with that way of his of letting words slip out, 'cause contradicting him was as good as getting ready for a fight.

'"Go fuck yourself!" concluded Menaplenty, falling to the floor and wrapping himself up in the blanket like someone who's getting ready for bed.

'You could still see the shape of the other going up and down the rubbish heaps and walking in a direction which wasn't towards the hut. But I, who was sure about what he was scheming, got very uneasy and wanted to go after him to make him think twice. But I'd surely have had to fight with him and hardly had the strength to stand upright, let alone to scrap with such a brute who wasn't capable of taking all the drink he had in his body.

'Menaplenty seemed to be starting to doze off. The booze had him mumbling his way quietly through those songs women belt out in the processions… But because I felt so uneasy I couldn't join in, 'cause if I went along with what I thought was going to happen then I was going to have a burden on my conscience now and for the rest of my life. It was well known, 'cause of other cowards and layabouts who'd already tried the same thing, that Socorrito was very strong and brave, able to defend herself from assaults. And on the other hand, as I knew very well that Gobs was an animal were it not for the blessed soul that God put into him to no avail, I was well aware that if his imagination could scheme to throw on the scented water to make him smell like a fancy gentleman, then he was the kind of man who could do any reckless thing.

'After walking some more, he disappeared into the darkness. As far as I'm concerned, and in spite of everything I was thinking about, the light-headedness meant that as soon as I fell to the ground I began to see him just as if I was dreaming... The moon had disappeared a while beforehand. The sky was clear and everything freezing over. A cloud of smoke or mist was rising up from the ground and stayed low and you could begin to see, along the top of Montalegre hill, the first light, still quite foggy, of the dawn. Between the heaps of rubbish, the pools of frozen rain water could be seen, and flashes of gigantic mice went by, romping around in the rubbish right next to us, sometimes running right over me as if we were dead.

'I felt as if at that very moment I was going to die. I couldn't work out if the pain was to do with my such poorly-treated body, or the "feeling" which was coming over me in a different way, but whatever it was, I now felt like I was on my last legs, and by now neither thing bothered me, and I let myself drift into that listlessness which seemed endless, as if I wanted to pull myself together and I couldn't for anything in the world, which was like going under, going under... and I still wanted with all my strength to cling to the memory of my mother, my kid, and I couldn't manage it, as if I was becoming completely empty and my mind was fading, and the "feeling" had never come over me in that way and without the urge to escape it like on other occasions, but wanting to let myself go wherever it took me, even if it meant death, which then no longer scared me...'

'...'

'Yes, Sir, he was still there, by my side. He was there, huddled in the blanket, with his chin plunged into his chest and his eyes closed. But, by the looks of it, he wasn't asleep. He'd stretch every now and again and would roll his head as if to rock himself to sleep and kept quietly mumbling the litanies that women sing in church... Then he turned, fell on all fours and emptied out everything he had in his body, moaning at every stage of the deluge. Then he turned face up and began scratching his belly, heaving with pain. As there was still little light, I lit a match and saw that his lips were bloody and his face white, shrivelled and covered in sweat... Day was dawning slowly, and I still couldn't make out the ground around me much in the middle of that rainy mist...

'It was then that a deafening shout was heard in the distance – a woman's voice. And I shot to my feet when the scream rang out again even louder. Then others followed, shorter, as if drowned out. Menaplenty was beside me, watching. The fright had driven away our pain.

'"What's that?" he said, trying to guess.

'"What do you think...? That brute who's with Socorrito." And with that I began to run as fast as my wounded feet would let me in search of the hut, which was some two hundred strides away sunk in a hollow in the ground, falling and getting up again on the heaps of rubbish. At that point Menaplenty overtook me, passing me by, brandishing a knife. I caught him by the arm to stop him, still running, and he turned towards me with a look on his face that I'd never seen before, which was exactly that of a man who doesn't know what he's doing.

'"That bastard is going to pay for everything and all at once...!"

'"Stop right there, Aladio! You'll be ruined 'cause of that swine...!"

'And it was then, when he was trying to get free, that he gave me this slash I've got on my wrist, and blood began to pour out of it.

'But I didn't let him go and we reached the hut together and together we went down the slope that surrounded it, at such a speed that we almost smashed against the door, which opened slightly.

'Gobs appeared, rising up out of a dark corner, with his trousers half up, the white skin of his belly visible down one side... And without saying a single word, Menaplenty strode towards him and in one strike sunk the knife into him right there and ripped it to one side, quickly removing it to strike again lower down, with the intention of wounding him in his privates, begging your pardon by the way. Gobs bent forward wanting to catch the blood oozing out with his hands, and that bundle of whitish things that spilt out of the enormous mouth of the wound. He still wanted to stay on his feet, but he couldn't, and fell on one side, curled up and clutching all that against himself...

Menaplenty leapt up and began to run... I ran too, but not very far, as the strength that I had left faded away with the horrible scene that I'd just witnessed. Aladio, who must have been running blind, went towards the edge of the lake, and I even saw him take a few steps on the ice, which when it cracked made a sound like glass shattering, and he sank, shouting until he disappeared...

'And this was how the sweepers found us, as I later... If I hadn't fallen unconscious 'cause of the pain I had in my body as much as from the blood that I was losing, I would've gone to notify the authorities myself, 'cause I've got nothing to do with the matter of these deaths, apart from them happening in front of me without me being able to do anything... I'm sorry about them dying, 'cause they were men just like me, but they more than deserved it and it's even like they got just what they were looking for...

'And with that, I've got nothing more to say, and may God have mercy on all of us...'

'...'

'Yes, Sir, yes. That's the very one. I haven't seen it very often, but it looks like Aladio Menaplenty's knife.'

'...'

'Of course, Sir. I say "it looks like" 'cause I hadn't seen it before and I didn't know that he carried it either, and I only saw it for a second in his hand, when we were running and when he struck me on the wrist. As to whether that is the "corpus delicti" or not, as you, Sir, point out, I can say that it might be, but I couldn't swear on it.'

'…'

'That is nonsense and even seems in bad faith, without any disrespect intended. I'm not a man for knives, everyone in town can tell you that… And please be kind enough to…!'

'…'

'No, Sir, I've got nothing and there's nothing wrong with me…'

'…'

'No, Sir, I don't shout nor do I have to, though I'm quite annoyed with you for daring to suggest that about the knife… Besides that, everything's been said, everything, and there's no need to keep upsetting people by asking them more than what they've said and know… I've told you everything and that's that…! 'Cause… When the "feeling" comes over me strongly, like now, which must be 'cause of my hunger or thirst, as it's been two days since I've eaten anything, or from poking into these matters things so much…! And what I want is to be left in peace 'cause I can't stand up any more… And, oh fuck it…!'

'…'

'No, Sir, no, not that please. I beg you for the love of God, for your children, for whoever is dearest to you… I'm begging you like this, on my knees… No… I don't want them to take me away! I'm not going! They're taking me to the police station…! Let me go! Murderers! Bastards…!'

Cipriano Canedo, or Cibrán, or Boar, or... might have still grabbed the knife from the top of the table as quick as a flash and sunk it between his own ribs... For there are people who are of such a nature that to be free of the "feeling" they have to kill it inside themselves... But it was never clear in the town if he died from the knifing or from the blows of the rifle butts that the two Civil Guard gave him right there.

My uncle, the "Minister", in spite of the fact that he was an establishment figure and, as is easily deduced from his office, particularly given to legal accuracy, used to mumble that they had taken Boar out of there with his forehead smashed in, and that the next day, when they were mopping up, they had found some snow drops beneath the table, "just like pus or matter, but they could also have been from the brains in our heads."

At least, that is what he said...

Other Galician translations published by Planet:

Them and Other Stories
Xosé Luís Méndez Ferrín
£6.75
0-9505188-4-0
Them and Other Stories brings together many of Xosé Luís Méndez Ferrín's short stories, from his earliest published work in 1958 to his latest collection *Arraianos* in 1991. Ferrín was a radical Galician nationalist and was imprisoned under Franco for his political beliefs and activities.

Things
Alfonso R. Castelao
£6.75
0-9505188-8-3
These very short stories, which approach prose poems in their lyric intensity, are Alfonso R. Castelao's contribution to a popular Galician art form. *Things* also features many of his accomplished illustrations, making the book an unusual creative whole.

Wounded Wind
Carlos Casares
£5.75
0-9540881-3-1
Wounded Wind portrays vividly the difficulties of life in Galicia, the poor, rainy north-western corner of Spain, in the 1950s and '60s. Its characters struggle with the darker side of existence, with solitude, frustration, injustice and its accompanying urge to violence and revenge.

available at www.planetmagazine.org.uk or use the QR code below